Disney

THE LION KING

ADAPTED BY ELIZABETH RUDNICK

BASED ON THE SCREENPLAY BY JEFF NATHANSON

BASED ON *THE LION KING* SCREENPLAY BY IRENE MECCHI
AND JONATHAN ROBERTS AND LINDA WOOLVERTON

PRODUCED BY JON FAVREAU, JEFFREY SILVER,
AND KAREN GILCHRIST

DIRECTED BY JON FAVREAU

DISNEY THE LION KING: THE BOOK OF THE FILM
A CENTUM BOOK 978-1-913072-38-4
Published in Great Britain by Centum Books Ltd
This edition published 2019
1 3 5 7 9 10 8 6 4 2

Centum Books Ltd, 20 Devon Square, Newton Abbot, Devon, TQ12 2HR, UK
books@centumbooksltd.co.uk
CENTUM BOOKS Limited Reg. No. 07641486
A CIP catalogue record for this book is available from the British Library
Printed in United Kingdom

To Jonathan Kast.

Your memory and love live on.

—E.R.

CHAPTER ONE

IN the moments before the sun rose over the horizon, the African plain was hushed. No birds sang. No animals called. The only sounds were the soft whisper of the breeze as it blew through the long grasses, still green in the early spring, and the distant thunder of the water cascading over Victoria Falls into the frothy pools below.

But as the sun's light began to break over the savannah, life began to stir.

It was slow at first, barely noticeable. A soft mew rising from the meerkat den. A rustle of feathers as the marabou storks lifted their long black wings and stretched their necks. Then faster and faster the sounds grew louder, merging into the song of the savannah. Cheetah mothers coaxed their young out into the sunlight with gentle nudges to their cubs' sides and quick licks to say hello. A pair of topis tapped their horns in greeting and then turned toward the grasslands, eager for their first meal of the day. Their brown bodies, marked with swaths of black, glimmered in the sun as it rose higher and higher.

Over the open plains, a herd of elephants began to march toward the watering hole, their long trunks swinging, the pads of their large feet leaving deep impressions on the dry ground. Near the top of a hill, a mother giraffe appeared, her baby following close behind, its head swiveling back and forth as it scanned the landscape for friends—and predators. Below, on a plain still covered with a thin layer of morning mist, a herd of gazelles leapt and played, the young ones jumping over brush with abandon and then spooking as an even larger herd of zebras passed by.

Even the smallest of life had awoken. On tree branches, ants began to march out of their holes and head to ground, careful to stay out of the way of the hungry guinea fowl. Tiny birds flew from branch to branch, the boldest occasionally swooping down to catch a ride on a passing elephant.

As all the animals of the savannah continued to wake, the sound grew to a crescendo until finally it broke with a loud trumpet from an elephant. But beneath the peace was a growing sense of excitement that every animal—from the largest to the smallest—felt. It was why, in almost perfect synchrony and complete harmony, they began to make their way to Pride Rock. The heart of their part of the savannah, Pride Rock was where Mufasa, the giant lion who had led the land for years, and his pride of lions lived. And on this day, he would introduce his kingdom to his son. It was a tradition that had been upheld for generations. Mufasa's family was well respected. He was a fierce and mighty lion, but he was kind, and he treated everyone—from the ants to the antelope—as important. In return, he had earned the respect of every animal family in the Pride Lands. And now they would show their respect by greeting his new son.

The sun had fully risen in the sky by the time all the animals arrived at Pride Rock. A hush fell over them as they raised their heads to look at the large rock jutting out over the savannah. It dominated the landscape, casting those nearest to it in shadow. For years, it had been the symbol of their kingdom, a natural amphitheater and gathering place. In the wet season it provided shelter, and in the dry season it was a refuge from the brutal sun. But most importantly, it was where Mufasa and his queen, Sarabi, lived with their pride of lions. Now it was a stage, and everyone was eager for the show to begin.

As they waited inside the cave tucked in the back of Pride Rock, Mufasa looked down at his queen. Beside her, their young son, Simba, slept peacefully, unaware of what was in store. His light brown body was relaxed, his sides rising evenly as he breathed in and out. Lowering her head, Sarabi gently nuzzled the young cub. Simba's eyes slowly opened. At the comforting sight of his mother and father, he let out a big yawn and then stretched. Mufasa smiled proudly, watching him. He had done many great things in his life, but the thing he was most proud of was this—his son, his queen, and the life he had created for them.

Hearing footsteps, Mufasa turned and his grin grew wider. His old friend and confidant Rafiki had arrived. Although the mandrill was a bit grizzled and bent, his eyes were still bright. He leaned on his wooden staff a little more than he once had, but his steps were still light. It had been Rafiki who'd introduced Mufasa to the kingdom when he was just a cub, as he would do now with Simba. Approaching each other, the two old friends exchanged a hug and then Mufasa stepped aside. It was time for the ceremony to begin.

Simba watched curiously as the monkey stepped in front of him. Seeing his wooden stick, the cub playfully tried to bat at it, missing and causing the adults around him to laugh. Rafiki nodded, pleased. It was a good sign for all of Pride Rock if Simba was curious and alert. Raising the stick above Simba, Rafiki shook it, causing red dirt to fall over the cub's head—and making the young cub sneeze.

Satisfied, Rafiki leaned down and carefully picked up Simba. Cradling him in one arm, he turned and slowly began to make his way out of the cave. Behind him, Mufasa and Sarabi followed, their bodies pressed close together. As they came out onto the rock, the sun went behind a cloud, as if not wanting to take away from the moment. Below, the animals leaned forward in anticipation. Step by step, Rafiki made his way toward the edge of Pride Rock until at last he stopped, mere inches from the steep drop. As the gathered animals watched from below, Rafiki lifted Simba up, up, up—until finally, he had raised baby Simba for all to see.

Instantly, the gathered animals erupted in noise: Elephants trumpeted. Zebras stomped their feet. Storks flapped their wings, and the cheetahs let out their own cries. Then the sun burst through the clouds, a beam of light falling right down onto the head of Simba—the future king.

The animals dropped their heads, bowing in respect.

Simba, still hanging from Rafiki's arms, looked down upon it all, unaware of the greatness of this moment. This was the way of life on Pride Rock. It was how it had always been and how it should always be. It was the Circle of Life, the way of the savannah. Through times of hardship and times of ease, the animals relied on one another and on the order of life to keep them going. Now it was Simba's turn to join that circle.

And while he didn't know it yet, someday it would be up to him to take his father's place and complete the circle—when he was king.

While nearly every animal in the savannah had come to greet their future king, there was someone missing. Someone whose presence, while not missed by others, was keenly felt by Mufasa. His brother, Scar, had missed the event.

Staring at the spot that had been kept open for him, Mufasa sighed. Once again, his brother had disappointed him. He had hoped that just this once Scar would step up, prove that he was above petty jealousies. But his hopes had been in vain. Scar had acted as he always had: bitter and resentful, angry to the core.

As Mufasa followed Rafiki and Sarabi back into the cave, his eyes wandered down to the shadows beneath Pride Rock, where Scar made his home. Anger began to replace the disappointment he felt. Yes, Scar had been born second; that was not Mufasa's fault. Yet, somehow, *he* had become the villain in the story of Scar's life. Mufasa knew the younger lion blamed him for his lower position. Scar was a fool and a bitter lion, content to slink about stirring discontent among the young lions and mocking and disrespecting his brother at every turn. Like he had done that day.

Nodding at his majordomo, a hornbill named Zazu, Mufasa signaled him over. Making sure not to bother

Sarabi or Simba, who was in the middle of a bath, Mufasa whispered his directions to Zazu. "Go and tell Scar I'm not pleased," he said, his deep voice commanding even in whisper. "I'll be down shortly to hear what his excuse is . . . this time." His orders given, he turned his attention back to his family. He wanted to spend a few more minutes enjoying them—not as a king, but as a father. Then he would go talk to Scar—not as his brother, but as his king.

CHAPTER TWO

Inside his cave, Scar sat in the shadows. He could hear the muffled sounds of celebration drifting in from outside. The cave shook as the animals paraded around Pride Rock, trumpeting and roaring in excitement over the presentation of beloved little Simba. Scar's eyes narrowed, and he swiped a paw angrily at the ground in front of him. Was it too much to ask for them to be just a tad quieter? So much fuss for such a tiny cub. It was disgusting and just like his big brother. The mighty king loved a good show.

Trying to tune out the noise, Scar focused on a much more pressing task—his afternoon snack. Lowering himself into a crouch, he shifted farther back into the shadows and waited. Within moments, the cave grew eerily quiet, as though Scar had stopped breathing and moving altogether. Out on the savannah, the skill would have made him a mighty hunter. But the scar on his eye had made him ineffectual to his father, so he had never been brought along on hunts, never shown the way of the hunter. Inside his cave, however, he was the mightiest of warriors. No one judged his weak appearance: his ribs always protruding no matter how much he ate; his mane mangy and thin; his coat mottled and turning prematurely gray; his mismatched eyes—one bright, the other clouded and scarred. No, inside his cave, he was the king.

And he was about to get a meal.

A mouse, lulled into a false sense of security by the quiet, scampered out into the center of the cave. He lifted his nose to the air and his whiskers twitched, his little eyes darting back and forth. Convinced he was well and truly alone, he scurried forward, his nose pressed to the ground as he searched for a crumb. Focused on his task, the little mouse didn't notice as a shadow rose up on the cave wall behind him.

Slowly, Scar got to his feet, his hackles raising and his eyes narrowing as he fixed on his prey. This was his favorite part. The moment before he pounced—when he was steps ahead of his victim. Mufasa had always been the brawnier of the two, but Scar—he was the brainier. And he loved a good game of cat and mouse. Inching forward, he was soundless, the pads of his giant paws barely touching the cold hard ground of the cave. When he was almost on top of the mouse, he lifted one paw up. It hung in the air above the mouse for a second and then slammed down, trapping the creature against the wall.

A sneer of pleasure came over Scar's face. Behind his paw he could feel the mouse frantically trying to escape. But there was nowhere to go. Lifting his paw, he brought his nose down right in front of the frightened creature. "Life's not fair, is it, my little friend?" he said. He was so close to the mouse that his breath made the small animal's fur move. "While some are born to feast, others spend their lives in the dark—begging for scraps. The way I see it, you and I are exactly the same." He lowered his head still closer, silently laughing at the irony of comparing himself to a mouse. But it was true. They were the same. They were both stuck in their situations. And while he may have been born into the proudest of families, Scar was seen as no mightier than a mouse. Sighing, he went on. "We both want to find a way out. . . ."

Lifting the mouse up by his tail, Scar let him squirm for a moment. He would never grow tired of the pleasure it gave him to make the weak suffer. And why should he? He was the weak one in his family. And look at what they had done to him: cast him aside, treated him like dirt while they showered Mufasa with praise and attention. Scar would never be king. That much was a given, especially now that the little brat had been born. But it didn't mean he couldn't find some source of joy—even if it came in the form of hurting creatures too small to fight back.

With renewed focus, Scar opened his mouth and began to lower the mouse down. He was just about to snap his jaws shut when he heard flapping wings. A moment later, the unmistakable sound of Zazu's voice echoed throughout the cave.

"The king approaches!" the hornbill cried. "This is NOT a drill!"

At the word *king,* Scar's grip on the mouse loosened. It was just for a moment, but it was all the mouse needed. Jumping free of Scar—and away from his still open mouth—the mouse sprinted toward the small hole through which he had come. Before Scar could even let out a growl of frustration, his snack had disappeared.

In its place stood Zazu.

Sitting down, Scar eyed the nervous bird. He hated Zazu—almost as much as he despised Mufasa. The bird felt that just because he was Mufasa's trusted aide he could go anywhere and say anything. It was irritating. As was his habit of constantly being nervous and in a state of fear—not that anyone could touch the bird without punishment from the king.

Feeling the lion's gaze on him, Zazu scanned the cave. His nose dipped down as he took in the dirty surroundings, the matted thin bed in the corner, and the remains of Scar's last snack. Then he looked up at Scar. "His Majesty has requested an audience," he announced. "Upon his entrance you will rise and genuflect."

Scar ignored him, looking instead at the spot in the cave wall where the mouse had gone. "Zazu," he said, dragging out the hornbill's name and managing to sound completely put off, "you've made me lose my lunch."

Zazu did not seem concerned. "You'll answer to Mufasa for missing the ceremony this morning!"

Instantly, Scar was on his feet. He began to move toward the bird, his head lowered and his lips pulled back in a snarl. If Zazu thought he could just fly in and command him to bow and act sorry, he was a stupider bird than Scar had believed. As he got closer, he licked his lips hungrily.

"Scar—" Zazu said, beginning to back up. "Don't look at me like that!"

"Are you hungry, Zazu?" Scar asked, not stopping. "Perhaps we could have a *bite* together?"

Hearing the hunger—and hatred—in Scar's voice, Zazu lifted up off the floor of the cave. He could wait for Mufasa outside just as easily as inside. But before he could turn and fly away, Scar lunged forward, blocking the entrance to the den. His body shut out the sunshine and cast the entrance into shadow.

Zazu shivered. "You can't eat me!" he said, trying to keep his voice from shaking—and failing.

In answer, Scar snapped his jaws. With a squawk, Zazu lifted into the air, barely avoiding having his beak bitten in half. Below him, Scar snapped again and again, the sound echoing and bouncing off the walls of the den.

"SCAR!" Backlit by the sun, Mufasa filled the entire

entrance to the den. His massive mane looked the color of fire, but his eyes were cold as they stared down at Scar.

"Well, look who's come down to mingle with the commoners," Scar finally said, eyeing his brother and Zazu with disdain. He lifted a paw and began to groom himself.

"Come out here!" Mufasa ordered. He knew exactly what Scar was doing. He was trying to act as though he didn't have a care in the world. But Mufasa knew different. He knew Scar hadn't shown because of one reason and one reason alone: jealousy. Stepping back, he waited for the other lion to follow him.

Slowly, Scar slunk out in the sunshine. He squinted, unaccustomed to the bright light. He began to walk around Mufasa, checking to be sure the king hadn't brought anyone else along with him. But Mufasa was alone.

"Sarabi and I didn't see you at the presentation of Simba," Mufasa finally said. He lifted his head toward the top of Pride Rock, high above them. His body was relaxed but his tone made his displeasure clear. He didn't bother to look at Scar, instead just waiting to hear the excuse.

Pausing in front of a large rock, Scar flicked out a long, sharp talon and began to run it over the hard surface. Zazu grimaced at the painful noise, but Mufasa didn't flinch. "Was that today?" Scar said. "Must have slipped my mind." He shrugged. "Of course, I meant no disrespect toward His Majesty. Or Sarabi. As you know, I have tremendous respect for the queen. . . ." His voice trailed off, his omission blatant.

Zazu's head swiveled back and forth between the two brothers. It was never comfortable being in the same area as them, but now it was downright frightening. He could feel the rage practically boiling off Mufasa, and he could smell the indifference on Scar. Clearing his throat, the hornbill took a step forward. "As the king's brother, you should have been first in line," he pointed out, voicing what Mufasa had obviously been thinking.

Scar lifted an eyebrow, the movement pulling at his

scar and making him look even meaner than usual. Was Zazu joking? Did he not see the irony in what he'd said? "I *was* first in line," he reminded them. "Or don't you remember. That is, until the precious prince arrived." Tired of the conversation, Scar turned to walk away. He had more important things to do than be chastised by a bird and his birdbrained brother—like find his runaway lunch.

"Don't turn your back on me, Scar!"

At the sound of Mufasa's voice, Scar reeled back around. He had had enough. "Oh, no, Mufasa," he snarled. "Perhaps you shouldn't turn your back on me."

"Is that a challenge?" Mufasa roared. Lifting his head, he puffed out his chest and squared off against Scar. For a long, tense moment, the two lions stood there, eyes locked, until finally, Scar lowered his head and began to back away.

He was small, but he was not foolish. There was no point in fighting. "I wouldn't dream of challenging you." He stopped, and then added, "Again."

Mufasa's hackles rose and a growl began at the

back of his throat. But before he could snap, Zazu flew in between them. "A wise decision!" he said to Scar. "You are no match for His Royalness!"

Scar shrugged. "Well, as far as brains go, I've got the lion's share. But when it comes to brute strength, I'm afraid my big brother will always rule."

"Not always," Mufasa said, correcting him. "One day it will be my son who rules. Simba will be your king."

"Then long live the king," Scar said. Turning back toward his den, he slunk away, disappearing into the darkness.

Watching him go, Mufasa let out a sigh. That was not how he had wanted things to go. True, he had been angry that Scar had skipped the ceremony, but a piece of him—however small—had hoped that maybe there had been a good reason. That perhaps with a new generation born, they could put aside their past. But clearly that was not going to happen.

"What am I going to do with him?" Mufasa said

as he and Zazu began to make their way back to the top of Pride Rock.

"Well, here's a thought," Zazu said, not hesitating to offer up his dream solution. "Why not drag him away with your massive teeth and claws?"

Mufasa tried not to laugh. It was no secret that the hornbill despised Scar. He wasn't sure if it was because of Zazu's loyalty to his king or the fact that Scar was so messy. Zazu despised disorder.

"What?" Zazu said. "We both know he should have been expelled from the Pride Lands long ago."

Mufasa's smile faded. "He's my brother, Zazu," he said, shaking his head. "This is his home. As long as I'm king, that will never change." *No matter how difficult Scar makes it for me,* he added silently.

CHAPTER THREE

Time passed as it does on the savannah: the Circle of Life continued to spin as dry weather gave way to wet. Lake beds evaporated and then filled. Herds thinned out and then grew bigger. Sunshine baked the ground and then rain drowned it. And through it all, the lions of Pride Rock watched as their young prince grew bigger and bolder.

The long days of napping in his mother's paws were over for Simba. His fur had darkened from days playing in the sun, and his belly had lost its chubbiness and become lean from constant activity. His eyes, bright and inquisitive, never stopped moving and he rarely stopped talking. Only when sleep overcame him did he finally stop, but even in slumber his paws moved as he dreamed of chasing antelope across the savannah.

Waking from a particularly great dream involving helping his father save a family of topis from a flood, Simba stretched out his paws and arched his back. Then, lifting his head, he let out a loud yawn. Nearby, one of the other cubs stirred in his sleep but then settled, nestling back into his mother's side. Simba waited for one more second, hoping to perhaps rouse a playmate, but after another yawn—intentionally louder this time—he realized he was going to have to find someone else to keep him company. Then his eyes widened. He didn't need someone to play with. He had totally forgotten what today was! Today he was supposed to spend time with his dad, just like in his dream!

Getting to his feet, he began to bounce and leap

over the sleeping lionesses and their cubs until he reached the front of the den, where his mother and father slept. Grabbing hold of Mufasa's tail, Simba pulled himself up and then began to crawl over the sleeping lion's massive back. While Simba had grown substantially since his introduction ceremony, atop his father he still looked tiny. Reaching Mufasa's head, he flopped down on it and began to bat at the large lion's ear. "Dad—you awake?" he said. "Dad . . ."

In answer, Mufasa let out a loud snore.

So, you think pretending to snore will fool me? Simba thought. His eyes narrowed and filled with mischief. *Well, we'll see about that.* Leaning farther over so his mouth was now directly in front of Mufasa's ear, he began to shout. "Dad! WAKE UP, DAD! DAD! DADADADADAD!"

Sarabi opened one eye and looked at her son. Seeing that he wasn't bleeding, hurt, or in need of anything pressing, she closed the eye once more. "Your son is awake," she said, her voice thick with sleep.

Beside her, Mufasa shook his head, giving Simba a

ride in the process. “Before sunrise he’s your son!” he said, not even bothering to open his eyes. This wasn’t the first time he had awoken to the shouts—or teeth—of his precocious son.

“Come on, Dad,” Simba whined. “Let’s go! You said I could patrol with you today! And today has started. You promised!” Charging down his father’s mane, Simba threw himself to the end and hung there, clinging to the tough hair with his small claws. “You up?” he asked, only this time he was not whining—he was smiling. Because he could see that while his dad might not have liked it, he was well and truly awake.

Slowly, the king rose to his feet. Then he, too, let out a yawn. But unlike Simba’s tiny one, this yawn bounced off the walls of the den and startled more than a dozen sleeping lions awake. “Let’s do this,” he said, shaking off the last of the sleep and giving Sarabi a quick nuzzle. Then, together, he and Simba walked out of the den and into the early morning sunshine. Behind them, Sarabi watched, a smile on her lips. She knew Mufasa’s hesitation was just an act. There was nothing he loved more than spending time with Simba. And if that gave her a few more moments of peace and quiet, it just made it all the sweeter.

"So, what's first?" Simba said, looking out at the savannah stretched before them. "Give orders for the hunt? Chase away evil intruders?"

Rather than answer, Mufasa began to walk ahead. But instead of going down the rocks toward the ground below, he began to walk up to the very top of Pride Rock. Simba raced to catch up, leaping and falling as he struggled over the steep rock face. "Dad!" he shouted. "You're going the wrong way!"

Still Mufasa did not answer. Slowly and steadily he climbed. A few moments later, Simba arrived, out of breath and very confused. Looking over, he saw his father sitting with his back to the rock, his eyes focused on the horizon and the sun as it climbed ever higher. Simba walked over and sat down on the plateau next to him. He waited for a minute—which in Simba time felt like hours—and then, finally, he couldn't take it anymore. "What are we doing? There's nothing up here!" he said.

Mufasa shook his head. "Look, Simba," he said, his deep voice serious. "Everything the light touches is our kingdom."

Following his father's gaze, Simba took in the horizon and all the land that lay in front of it. His eyes grew wide. "Wow," he said softly. "You rule all of that?"

"Yes," Mufasa said with a nod. "But a king's time as ruler rises and falls like the sun. One day, Simba, the sun will set on my time here—and will rise with you as the new king."

Simba nodded, hearing what his father was saying but not quite processing it. There was something so serious, so sad, in his father's tone and it made him shiver unexpectedly. They had never talked like this before. And while he couldn't explain it, it made him sad, too, to hear Mufasa speak of his own time ending. But then, as quickly as the flash of sadness came, it went, replaced by a sudden realization. "Wait," Simba said, perking up. "You're saying all of this will belong to me?"

"It belongs to no one," Mufasa corrected, with a shake of his large head. "But it will be yours to protect. A great responsibility." He turned his gaze from the horizon and looked down at Simba. The young cub knew nothing of responsibility, but he would all too soon. Lions grew up fast in the Pride Lands and he needed his son to understand what was at stake.

For a moment, Simba just stared out at the savannah, his mouth open in awe. "No way," he finally said. "Are you sure? Everything the light touches? Those trees and the watering hole and that mountain and"—he paused, scanning the horizon for still more—"beyond those shadows?"

Mufasa followed his son's gaze to the farthest point on the horizon, where the sun barely touched and the land seemed cast in permanent shadow. He shook his head. "For now, you must not go there, Simba," he warned.

"But I thought a king can do whatever he wants," Simba said, looking confused. "Take any territory."

Mufasa sighed. "While others search for what they can take, a true king searches for what he can give."

Turning, Mufasa began to make his way back down Pride Rock. Simba paused, watching as his father easily maneuvered over the sharp rocks. *Someday I'm going to be just like him,* Simba thought. *And then I'll be able to go anywhere I want and nothing will scare me. Not even the shadowlands.*

With a determined nod, Simba began to follow Mufasa. For a while, father and son walked in companionable silence, each lost in his own thoughts. As they made their way through the Pride Lands, Mufasa pointed out the small, almost secret sights of the kingdom: the caverns carved out of ancient rock that were home to long-horned bulls; the grove of trees that supplied food to one herd of elephants. Simba took it all in, his eyes wide. Watching a pair of bulls fight, the sound of their clashing horns bouncing off the cavern walls, he pressed himself closer to his father.

He was going to be brave and nothing was going to scare him—someday. For now, he still liked having his father by his side.

As they moved onto one of the longer parts of the flat savannah, Simba saw a herd of antelope leaping and bounding toward them. His heart began to pound and he looked up at his father, hopeful for a fun chase. But Mufasa shook his head.

"Everything you see exists together in a delicate balance," he said. "As king, you need to understand that balance and respect all the creatures—from the crawling ant to the leaping antelope."

Simba cocked his head. "But Dad—don't we eat the antelope?"

"Yes, Simba," Mufasa said. Simba started to nod proudly but stopped when he saw his father wasn't done. "Let me explain. When we die, our bodies become the grass, and the antelope eat the grass. And so, we are all connected to the great Circle of Life."

"Sire!"

Hearing the unmistakable voice of Zazu, father and

son turned and looked back in the direction of Pride Rock. Zazu was flying toward them, his colorful beak seeming even brighter in the sun.

"Morning, Zazu," Mufasa said when the hornbill had landed in front of them. "Do you have the morning report?"

Zazu gave a curt nod. "Yes, sire!" he said. Then, puffing out his chest, he began: "Ten flamingos are taking a stand. Two giraffes were caught necking. . . ."

As Zazu continued his report, he turned away from Mufasa. Catching Simba's eye, Mufasa crouched down and signaled for Simba to do the same. "Ready for some fun?" he whispered, motioning with his eyes in Zazu's direction. "Stay low to the ground."

His belly just brushing the tips of the grass, Simba nodded excitedly. He eyed his target. "I got this," he said softly.

"Check the wind," Mufasa went on, helping his son. But the cub was a natural. Even as Mufasa offered advice, Simba was one step ahead. He lifted his nose and checked his shadow to make sure it wouldn't give him away, all the while not moving a muscle as he readied to pounce.

Zazu, completely oblivious to his part in the hunt, rambled on. "The buzz from the bees is that the leopards are in a bit of a spot. The tick birds have been tweeting again in the middle of the night—they can't stop." As Zazu went on, Simba inched a little closer. His tail swished ever so slightly and his nose twitched. The wind was on his side. Still, he waited, letting Zazu finish. "The cheetah stole the baboon's dinner—and now the baboons are going ape. Of course, I always say, cheetahs never prosper!" The bird started to laugh at his own pun but stopped as he was tackled from behind.

Rolling over, he looked up to find himself beak to nose with Simba.

Mufasa let out a loud laugh as Simba proudly stood on his "catch." Hemming and hawing, Zazu took to the air, shaking off his feathers. He looked utterly put out—and was about to point out that he was the king's aide, not the prince's plaything, when he spotted something in the distance. He squinted, wanting to be sure of what he saw before he sounded the alarm. But there was no doubt what it was. "Sire!" he shouted. "Hyenas in the Pride Lands! They're on the hunt!"

Instantly, Mufasa was on alert. The laughter died, and his expression grew fierce. Watching the transformation, Simba took a nervous step back.

"Can you see Sarabi?" Mufasa asked Zazu.

The hornbill nodded. "She and the lionesses are chasing them down."

Pleased with the answer, Mufasa began to run. Sarabi and the other lionesses would keep the hyenas away long enough for him to get there. Then it would be up to him to remind the hyenas—in a not-so-gentle way—that they were not to set foot in the Pride Lands, per their agreement. He had run just a few feet when he came to a sudden stop. Turning, he called back to Zazu. "Take Simba home!" he ordered.

"Dad!" Simba protested. "Let me come! I can help!"

Mufasa shook his head. "No, Son," he said. "You stay with the other cubs, where it's safe." His message delivered, he turned and began to race over the savannah. In moments, he was a mere speck in the distance.

Watching him go, Simba hit the ground with his paw. His father was wrong. He was *not* a cub. He was almost a grown-up lion and he should be helping his father save the Pride Lands. That was his duty. But no. Now he had to go back to Pride Rock and hang out with the babies—and Zazu. It just wasn't fair.

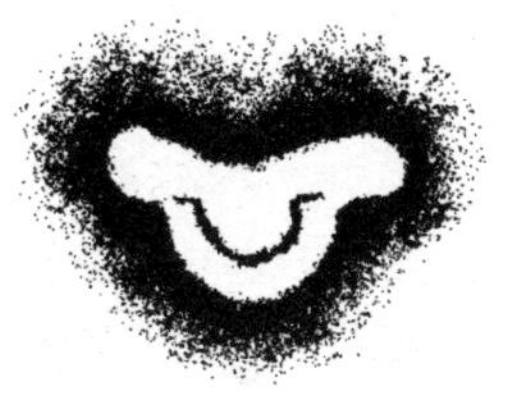

CHAPTER FOUR

Simba sat at a distance, watching as several lion cubs laughed and chased each other around the area in front of the den. He scowled as one cub tackled another and then playfully bit the other cub's ear. A part of him wanted to join in their fun, but another part of him was still fuming from being left behind. *Maybe,* he thought, *if I show Dad what a good hunter I'm becoming, he'll take me with him next time.*

With a determined nod, Simba scanned the

area. He needed something to hunt. He saw Zazu perched on one of the higher rocks. Possible . . . but not great. He wanted a different challenge, and since he had already tackled Zazu that morning, he kept looking. The other cubs were a possibility . . . but then he would have to tell them what he was doing, and they would probably want to join him. Finally, his eyes landed on a beetle moving over the rocks. Its black back glistened in the sun and it was moving at just the right pace.

Slipping away from the rock, he crouched low, just like his father had taught him. Then he began to inch forward. He was so focused on tracking the beetle that he didn't even realize he was moving down the rocks, away from the den and toward the bottom of Pride Rock. He had just decided to make his move and pounce when a voice from behind startled him.

"If you wish to kill something, you might want to stay downwind."

Whirling around, Simba saw his uncle slowly amble

out from the darkness of his cave. He paused in the entrance, half his body still in shadow.

"I know how to hunt, Uncle Scar," Simba said. To prove himself, he turned and pounced—completely missing the beetle and instead slamming headfirst into a rock.

Behind him, Scar raised an eyebrow. "Let's hope we're never attacked by a beetle," he said, his voice dripping with sarcasm. Then he nodded up toward the top of Pride Rock. "Go back to your den, Simba. I don't babysit." With a swish of his tale, he headed back into the cave.

Watching him go, Simba cocked his head. "Babysit?" he repeated, following his uncle inside. He didn't need a babysitter. "I'm going to be king of Pride Rock. My dad showed me the whole kingdom—said I'm going to rule it all."

"Is that so?" Scar said, sounding unimpressed.

Simba nodded. Moving closer to his uncle, he glanced around the cave. He had never been inside his uncle's den before. He wrinkled his nose. It was dirty and smelled . . . funny. It was cold, too. Down at the bottom of Pride Rock, it didn't get the warmth of the sun the way Simba's own den did. He shivered, suddenly wishing he hadn't strayed quite so far. But then he remembered that morning. He wasn't a little cub anymore. He didn't need to go running home. "Think about it," he said, focusing his attention back on his uncle. "When I'm king, I'll have to give you orders. Tell you what to do, where to go. How weird is that?"

"You have no idea," Scar said. Coming closer, he looked down at Simba. "So . . . your dad showed you the whole kingdom?" he asked. Simba nodded. "Did he show you the shadows beyond the northern borders?"

Simba stopped nodding and looked up at his uncle in surprise. How had Scar known that he'd asked his dad about that very spot? Simba frowned. Had Zazu told him? Had Zazu told everyone that his dad didn't trust him? His frown deepened. "He said I can't go there. Ever."

To his surprise, Scar nodded. "And he's absolutely

right! An elephant graveyard is no place for a young prince—" Scar stopped suddenly, looking guilty. "Oops."

"Elephant graveyard?" Simba repeated, his eyes wide. "Whoa!" No wonder his father wanted him to stay away—it was probably the coolest place ever. Full of big bones and all sorts of stuff he had never seen. Then he cocked his head. But how could a place like that really be all that dangerous? Who would want to hang out with a bunch of bones? Still . . . it would be pretty amazing to see it.

"Oh, dear," Scar said, clearly reading the excitement on his nephew's face. "I've said too much. Well, I suppose you'd have found out sooner or later. You being king and all."

Simba looked up at his uncle with awe. "You've been there?" he said. Scar nodded, and Simba's eyes grew even wider. His father had always told him to leave Scar alone. But now that he was there, talking to him, Scar didn't seem all that bad. In fact, he was the only one who seemed to realize Simba would be king someday and maybe deserved to know some things.

But just as Simba started to feel like he and Scar could be friends, his uncle shook his head.

"We've all been there. And it's no place for a cub," he said.

At the word *cub,* Simba grimaced. But Scar's next words distracted him all over again. "All those rotting bones and burning pools of oozing mud . . ."

"Rotting bones . . . Oozing mud?" Simba felt as though he were about to leap out of his skin. He wanted to go there—now.

Scar held up a paw. "Promise me you'll stay away, Simba," he said solemnly. "Now you run along." Reaching out, he gave Simba a little push. Simba tried to turn back but his uncle didn't budge. Lowering his head, Simba sighed and began to make his way up toward Pride Rock. Just as he reached the path, he heard Scar call out his name. Turning back hopefully, Simba saw his uncle still standing where he had left him. "Remember," Scar called out. "It's our little secret. Your Majesty." With a nod, the older lion turned and slunk back into his den.

Our little secret, Simba repeated to himself. He could keep the secret. He wouldn't tell anyone that he had spent time with Scar or that he had learned what lay in the shadows near the horizon. Well, he wouldn't tell *almost* anyone. Because there was someone he definitely had to tell—when he convinced her to go with him to see the graveyard!

Nala lay on her stomach, itching to move. Her mother, Serafina, was in the middle of giving her a bath—and Nala *hated* baths. She wanted to be out playing with the other cubs, or even better, she wanted to find her best friend, Simba, and do something with him. Maybe go to the watering hole? Play a game of catch the tail on the lion cub? Practice pouncing? But instead, she had gotten snatched up by her mother and was now being forced to sit still while every inch of her golden fur was licked. Her mother liked to pay special attention to the white markings that made Nala's coat unusual—and beautiful.

Nala had to admit, though, it felt kind of nice. It was part of her daily routine, and while she sometimes wished she didn't have to do everything her mother told her to do, being a cub was mostly pretty great. It meant she could play when she wanted and get meals whenever she was hungry, and she could always sleep tucked up next to her mother inside the safety of the den. Being part of Mufasa's pride was special, and Nala knew that. It was what she had been taught since she was born. Only days younger than Simba, she and the future king had grown up together, and when he was taught a lesson, so was she. When he learned about the kingdom, so did she. It was almost as if her mother had been grooming her to be a royal. The thought made Nala laugh. Her? Royalty? That would be the day.

Hearing footsteps at the entrance to the den, Nala lifted her head. A smile spread over her face as she saw Simba's curious eyes scanning the den for her. She tried to signal to him, but Serafina pushed her paw down and licked harder. Luckily, Simba spotted her anyway.

"Nala!" Simba shouted as he raced over. "Come on! We have to go!"

"Where?" Nala said, trying to move and not having much luck.

Simba looked like he was going to jump out of his skin with excitement. Nala smiled as he danced in front of her, unable to stop his tail from twitching. His brown eyes were wide and his ears moved back and forth. He turned and pointed out of the den. "The watering hole!" he said, as if that were the obvious answer.

Before Nala could reply, Serafina shook her head. "Nala is having her bath," she said. To prove it, she resumed her licking.

"And it's time for yours."

Looking over, Nala saw Simba's mother, Sarabi, entering the den. Her own coat was dusty, but it didn't stop her from looking regal. She was a huge lioness, bigger than Serafina, with a wide head and large, knowing eyes. Nala had always been a little in awe of her. As queen, it was Sarabi's duty to provide for the lionesses and cubs. Mufasa helped, but Sarabi carried the majority of the weight on her strong shoulders. Nala knew her mother was Sarabi's best friend and right hand when it came to hunting. She hoped to someday be as fierce as both of them.

As Simba protested, Sarabi lifted him by the scruff of his neck and sat down on a nearby ledge. She began to lick him, her rough tongue ridding his fur of the dirt from his earlier adventure outside. Finally, he broke free. "See—all clean," he said, twirling in front of Sarabi. "Can we go?"

Sarabi raised her nose and sniffed the air.

"There's no hyenas," Simba said, realizing what she was doing. "You just chased them all off!"

Nala looked up to see if Sarabi would snap at Simba, but instead, she saw the lioness trying to hide a smile. Simba *was* hard to argue with. "Just to the watering hole—no further," she finally said, nodding in agreement.

"Go through the high grass," Serafina said, releasing Nala from her grasp. Jumping to her feet, Nala raced over to join Simba. She waggled her eyebrows in excitement, and together, the cubs turned to go.

But Sarabi wasn't done yet. "Stay downwind," she said. "And one more little thing . . . Zazu will be going with you."

At the same time, Nala and Simba let out groans of dismay. Taking the bird with them would take all the fun out of whatever adventure Simba had in mind. Because if Nala knew one thing, it was Simba. And she knew he was up to something. He would tell her, but with Zazu along, she would probably have to wait. . . .

CHAPTER FIVE

"So, where are we *really* going?"

As they had been told to, Simba and Nala were making their way through the high grass of the savannah. The sun warmed their backs and the ground underfoot was still soft from the wet season rains. Too soon, it would bake under the unrelenting sun, turning the ground hard and painful to walk on. But for now, it was enjoyable. And other than the sound of Zazu's off-key humming as he flew above them, it was also quite peaceful.

At Nala's question, Simba looked over, surprised. She was always doing that to him—guessing when he had something up his sleeve. "How did you know?" he whispered, not wanting to catch Zazu's attention.

Nala raised an eyebrow. "You hate the water," she said.

Simba nodded. She had a point. He did hate the water, and he usually had to be dragged kicking and screaming to the watering hole. "I heard about this place, Nala," he said. "The most incredible, amazing—"

"Just tell me where!" Nala said, cutting him off.

Simba smiled. That was one of the things that made Nala his best friend—she was always up for anything. "An elephant graveyard."

"How far is it?" she asked.

"Not far," Simba said, though he realized he wasn't exactly sure how far away the shadows were. "But don't worry—everyone's been there."

CHAPTER FIVE

For the first time, Nala looked slightly nervous. "What if we get lost?"

Simba pushed ahead, brushing the grass out of his way. It was thinning out as they approached the watering hole. He didn't want to admit it out loud, but he had wondered the same thing. Getting lost sounded scary. . . . Still, he couldn't sound weak or scared in front of Nala. After all, he *was* the future king. And Scar *had* said everyone had been there. There was probably a path or something. "Relax, Nala," he said. "I patrolled the entire kingdom this morning with my dad. There's nothing to worry about."

"Well, there is *one* thing." Nala lifted her head toward Zazu.

The bird was flying in circles, anxiously scanning the area in front of, behind, and to the sides of him—repeatedly. "We have an imminent threat!" he suddenly screeched. Both cubs stopped in their tracks. "Something is approaching. Wait—" Zazu's eyes narrowed and then his beak opened and shut. "That's my own shadow." Relieved they were safe, and not at all embarrassed by his overreaction, Zazu continued to monitor. "When we get to the water, I want you both to stay in the shallow end."

Ignoring the warning, the two cubs resumed walking. "How we getting rid of the dodo?" Nala whispered a moment later, leaning over.

Simba smiled. "Trust me," he said, puffing up his chest. "I got this. Just follow me to freedom—"

His words were cut off as he turned back and found himself face to face with Zazu. The bird had landed right in front of them without either of the cubs noticing. Simba's eyes narrowed. Maybe there *was* a reason his parents kept the bird around. . . .

"How lovely it is to see the future king with his future queen," Zazu said, looking back and forth between Simba and Nala. "I could just molt."

Simba cocked his head. "What do you mean, future queen?" he asked.

"Well, one day the two of you will be betrothed."

Zazu's words were met with blank stares. "Intended. Affianced!" he added.

"Simba, you speak bird?" Nala asked, not understanding what the hornbill was trying to say. Simba shook his head.

"Married!" Zazu translated in frustration. "One day you will be married—to each other."

For one long moment, Simba just stared at Zazu. Then he looked over at Nala. Then back at Zazu. Was the bird kidding? Married? To Nala? The thought of it seemed very strange to him. "Not going to happen, Zazu," he said, shaking his whole body as if that would get rid of the idea. "Nala and I are friends. And besides—she's afraid of rhinos!"

"And *he's* never eaten an impala!" Nala pointed out, clearly not into the idea, either.

Simba shot her a look. That wasn't entirely true. He had tried impala—once. He just didn't like it. Too gamey. Once more, he shook his head. They were never getting married, end of story. It didn't matter what the other did or didn't eat or like. They were friends. And they would be forever.

Zazu did not seem impressed. "A monarch who ignores tradition?" he said. "With an attitude like that, I'm afraid you'll be a pretty pathetic king!"

"Well, I'm not letting anyone tell me where to go, what to do, who to marry," Simba said, pushing past Zazu and continuing toward the watering hole. "There will never be a king like me!"

"Simba!" Zazu shouted after him. "You can't escape your destiny!"

"Just watch!" Simba shouted back. He wasn't just going to escape his destiny—he was going to escape the nosy hornbill, too.

Pushing through the rim of grass surrounding the watering hole, he was happy when he surprised a flock of flamingos. As they took to the air, their pink wings dripping with water, Simba laughed. Zazu could say silly things and tell him he was going to be pathetic as a king, but Simba had bigger plans. He was going to be a mighty king. No, not just a mighty king—the *mightiest* king. As he and Nala began to run around the water, ducking and weaving among the legs of elephants, hippos, and zebras, Simba heard Zazu's frantic reminders to stay in sight, and ignored them. He meant what he had said. No one was going to tell him what to do. He would roar as loudly as he wanted. He would run around and go anywhere he wished. He would be free! And as king, if he wanted to change the rules, he would.

Signaling to Nala, Simba jumped into a mud puddle, covering himself in the thick brown goo. Nala did the same. Emerging from the puddle, they slunk over and blended in among the elephants, who were also covered in mud to keep cool. Looking up, Simba saw that Zazu was still talking to him—though he clearly couldn't see him. With a flap of his wings, he turned, his back now toward Simba and Nala.

Seeing his chance, Simba raced away from the elephants and along the bank of the watering hole, heading toward the far side. Nala followed close behind. They just needed to get to that side and then they would be closer to the Elephant Graveyard—and hopefully farther from Zazu.

But suddenly, the hornbill turned and spotted them. "I know what you're doing!" he shouted. "You can't hide from me, Simba! It's my sworn duty to keep you safe!"

Simba stopped in his tracks. Zazu was right. He couldn't hide from Zazu forever. But there was another way. Quickly, he jumped up onto a ledge over the bank of the watering hole. Then—he jumped in!

The action startled the gathered animals. The zebras began to stomp their feet and the elephants swung their long trunks, splashing water everywhere. Almost instantly, Nala and Simba were washed clean—and Zazu was soaked through. As he tried to flap his waterlogged wings, Simba and Nala ducked between a pair of young hippos.

"You're coming home with me this instant!" Zazu said, still following them but falling farther behind.

Simba had had enough. He was going to be king. And a king didn't need a babysitter. Glancing ahead, he smiled. A huge flock of birds had landed in front of them. Letting out a roar, Simba took off, racing right at them. As the hundreds of brightly colored birds lifted into the air, they blocked Zazu—and gave Simba and Nala the chance they had been waiting for.

Before anyone could stop them, they raced away from the watering hole and straight toward the shadowy lands on the horizon.

"Simba!" Nala said when they finally stopped running. She was out of breath—both from the run and the thrill of the escape. She had never done anything that exciting before. "We really lost him!"

Simba lifted his head and smiled. "I know what you're thinking," he said. "The future king is a genius."

Nala gave him the stink eye. "You *can't* be serious," she said. "You never would have gotten halfway without the queen." She had been as shocked as Simba by the idea of them being "betrothed," as Zazu put it, but she *did* like the idea of being a queen. After all, Sarabi was as powerful as Mufasa—at least when it came to the hunt and ruling the lionesses. Mufasa listened to her and trusted her opinion.

"Aren't you forgetting something?" Simba said as they walked up the hill leading to a wide ridge. "There isn't going to be a queen."

Nala frowned at her friend. Her earlier thoughts vanished. He was right. She didn't want to be a queen—not if it meant marrying *him*. Ick! "I'd rather marry an aardvark," she said, shaking her head.

"Good luck finding one that will say yes," Simba said, laughing.

Nala stopped. She knew where this was going. The friendly teasing often led to this kind of moment. Simba was her best friend—and the future king—but sometimes he needed to be reminded he wasn't king *yet*. Slowly, she began to lower her body so her weight was on the backs of her legs. "Good luck getting out of here without a bruising," she said.

"Give it your best shot," Simba said, lowering his own body so the pair were now face to face.

CHAPTER FIVE

Nala waited. Simba always made the first move; he couldn't help himself. He was a show-off, and show-offs didn't like waiting. Sure enough, a moment later, Simba pounced.

Nala was ready. In one smooth move, she reared up on her hind legs and met the force of his pounce head-on. His momentum stopped, she quickly flipped him over onto his back. Throwing her own weight forward, she pinned him to the ground. Then she grinned. "I think you owe me an apology."

"Never!" Simba said, his voice wheezy as he struggled to push Nala off.

Finally slipping free, he once again rushed Nala. But once again, she flipped him over. Only this time, instead of landing on the flat ground of the ridge, they fell over it and began tumbling down the hill onto the other side. Over and over they fell, until they landed—Nala once more on top of Simba—at the bottom.

"I'm waiting . . ." Nala said, her tone teasing and her eyes bright.

But to her surprise, Simba didn't say anything.

Instead, his eyes were glued on something behind her. "Nala," he whispered. "What is that?"

Nala shook her head. "You're not going to trick me, Simba," she said. "I know there's nothing . . ." Her voice trailed off as she realized the sun was no longer warming her back and her voice was bouncing off rocks. She shivered. Then, slowly, she turned around.

Her eyes grew wide as she looked at what they had tumbled into. Jagged rocks lifted high into the sky, casting everything in shadow. The ground was hard and burned white. There were no trees, no shrubs, not even the call of a bird. All Nala could see were bones. Lots and lots of elephant bones.

"This must be it!" Simba said, getting to his feet. The initial fear Nala had seen in his eyes was gone, replaced with excitement. "Come on!" As he ran ahead, a thick layer of white dust drifted up into the air. Simba didn't seem to notice as he darted in and out of the bones, ducking under a huge set of ribs and leaping over a giant tusk.

Following slowly, Nala tried not to cringe. These

bones were all that was left of dozens of elephants. How had they come to be here? Why had they walked all this way? Was there some other reason they had ended up in this shadowy, desolate land? She loved to watch the elephant herds as they roamed the savannah. Next to the lions, of course, she thought they were the most majestic of all creatures. Seeing their bones made her sad. She shivered again. She had had enough. "Simba—we're way beyond the Pride Lands," she said.

Simba paused on top of a tusk and looked over at her. "We found it, Nala," he said, not sounding at all worried. In fact, he sounded proud. "You know what this means?"

"We can go home?" she answered hopefully.

Simba shook his head. "It means they won't treat us like cubs anymore!"

Nala opened her mouth to point out that they *were* cubs but stopped. She knew there was no point arguing with Simba. All he cared about was growing up and being king. To him, being taken care of and loved and fed were annoyances, whereas Nala, while she didn't love a bath, loved her mother and the den and her place in the pride. But Simba was her best friend and she wasn't going to leave him—even if she didn't agree with him. Shrugging, she started to follow him when, suddenly, a strange sound whistled through the wind. Both she and Simba stopped. "What was that?" Nala asked nervously.

"Just the wind moving through those rocks," Simba said. "Let's go check it out!"

Sighing, Nala watched as Simba bounded off. He was going to get them into trouble, she was sure of it. She just had to hope it wasn't any trouble they couldn't get out of, and that Mufasa wouldn't blame her . . . at least not entirely.

CHAPTER SIX

I don't know why Dad and Scar warned me about this place, Simba thought as he started to climb up a steep pile of rocks on the far side of the Elephant Graveyard. *Besides being dirty, it's not even a little scary. I bet they were just teasing me. I bet this is some sort of king's rite of passage or something. Well, I'll show them!*

Behind him, he could hear Nala muttering to herself. He had been surprised when she'd said they should go home. Usually Nala was all-in for an adventure. But the place had gotten her spooked. Or maybe she was just pouting because he had told her she couldn't even get an aardvark to marry her.

"Simba!" Nala shouted as he leapt off a particularly steep rock and landed in front of a narrow, dark cave. "Get down! It could be dangerous!"

"Danger?" Simba repeated, looking over his shoulder. "HA! I laugh in the face of danger!" Turning to look back at the cave, he let out a few more laughs. The sound echoed through the cave, bouncing off the walls and coming back at them. "You hear that, Nala?" he shouted.

Nala frowned. "Simba, come on!" she pleaded. "You proved how brave you are! The sun is going down and I'm not going to sit here and—"

Simba wasn't even listening. He was too busy laughing into the cave. He let out another series of "hahahas"—only this time, the sound that came back wasn't his own. It was the unmistakable—and terrifying—laugh of a hyena.

CHAPTER SIX

Before Simba could even turn to run or call out to warn Nala, a huge hyena charged out of the cave. His mouth was open wide, his long, pointy teeth covered in froth and saliva as he saw a fresh meal standing there. Just before he could bite Simba in two, Simba threw himself backward, tumbling down the rocks and landing, with a thud, right next to Nala.

As the two cubs watched, hyenas began to emerge from every direction. They came out of holes in the ground, from imperceptible gaps between rocks, and from caves Simba hadn't even noticed. In seconds, the cubs were surrounded. The hyenas' laughter bounced off the jagged rocks, filling the Elephant Graveyard with the terrible sound.

Suddenly, the larger group of hyenas parted, making way for two of their own to walk up to Simba and Nala. One of them could barely keep his tongue in his mouth and the other was scarred, his fur thin and his eyes hard.

The scarred one stepped forward, eyeing the cubs. "Well, look at this," he said. His voice was deep and raspy. "We weren't expecting guests today. Would you two cubs like to stay for dinner?"

But it wasn't Simba or Nala who replied.

"Yes! Great idea!" the hyena with the dangling tongue sneered. "You guys have to stay—we don't have much to eat, just some old bones to chew on—"

"Azizi," the larger hyena said, cutting him off, "I wasn't *actually* asking them to stay."

The hyena looked confused. "But you just said *stay*," Azizi pointed out. "Why are you lying to them?"

Simba shot Nala a look. They knew hyenas were not the brightest creatures, but Azizi was something else. Maybe there was a chance they could escape. If they could outsmart the hyenas, Simba figured they might just be okay.

But then the other hyena snarled, baring his fangs. He was clearly growing tired of his companion's stupidity. "Because they *are* dinner!" he said. "Understand?"

Azizi's eyes grew wide as he looked back and forth between the cubs. Then, slowly, he began to nod. "Oh,

I get it," he finally said. "That makes sense. But just to be clear—are they staying?"

"WE ARE EATING THEM!" the other hyena shouted, completely losing his cool. "RIGHT NOW!"

Simba and Nala began to inch backward as both hyenas turned toward them, mouths open. Simba gulped. He might have been wrong to think they could get out of this. They were trapped. And there was no way they could escape. . . .

"Nobody touches them!"

At the sound of the commanding voice, the hyenas froze. Looking up, Simba watched as a large female hyena slowly emerged from a cave. Unlike the bumbling duo in front of them, this hyena was strong, her coat clean and her eyes clear. She walked with her head up, and as she passed, the other hyenas bowed and backed away, making way for their queen.

Approaching the cubs, the large hyena looked down at them, studying them intently. Then a large grin broke over her spotted face. "Now, this is a meal I've waited my whole life for," she said, letting out a cackle. "What an unexpected treat—to eat the son of a king."

Simba swallowed nervously. This had to be Shenzi, the leader of the hyenas. He had heard of her. And clearly she knew who he was. Maybe that was a good thing? Maybe he could use it to his advantage. After all, if she was queen of the hyenas, perhaps there was some unspoken rule of respect for other royalty. Either way, he couldn't just stand there. Stepping in front of Nala, Simba puffed up his chest. "I *am* the future king," he said as loudly and bravely as he could. "Which means you can't do anything to me!"

"He's telling me what to do," Shenzi sneered. "His father's strength flickering inside. I wonder how all that bravery will taste. . . ." She took a step closer, her lips pulling back into a snarl as she bared her teeth. Simba backed up but she kept coming. He felt her breath on his cheek and saw the drool dripping from her fangs. He closed his eyes. . . .

"Let them go, Shenzi!"

Simba's eyes popped open. He had never in his life

been happier to hear the sound of Zazu's voice. Looking up, he watched as the hornbill swooped down and landed in front of him and Nala. Spreading his wings to their full width, Zazu blocked the cubs from Shenzi. "They made a mistake—a horrible mistake!" he went on. "But if you do this, you'll start a war with Mufasa!"

"Hyenas and lions have been at war since the beginning of time," Shenzi said, sounding unimpressed by Zazu's threat. "But Mufasa's bloodline will end here!" Moving forward, Shenzi signaled to the others and they, too, began to move. Zazu could give all the warnings he wanted. They were going to kill Simba—even if it meant war.

Lowering his wings, Zazu turned his head. "Run!" he shouted to Simba and Nala.

Simba didn't have to be told twice. Spinning on his back paws, he took off, with Nala right behind him.

Simba ran as fast and hard as he could. His heart pounded in his chest as he scrambled up and over rocks, trying to outrun the hyenas. He could hear Nala right behind him, her breath hitching as she, too, ran for her life.

He hadn't meant for things to turn out like this. He had just wanted to see what the Elephant Graveyard looked like and maybe have a story to tell his friends. He hadn't meant to put them in danger, and he *definitely* hadn't meant to become a hyena's dinner. If they made it out of here, he was going to be in big, big trouble. The thought spurred him on and his tiny paws moved faster. Glancing around, he frantically searched for a place to hide or a way to escape. But this was the hyenas' home. There was nowhere to hide.

Spotting a hole up ahead, Simba raced toward it. It wasn't the best option, but it had to be better than running out in the open. "In here!" he shouted over his shoulder to Nala just before he plunged headfirst into the opening.

Inside it was dark, and the smell of hyena was overwhelming. Simba's nose crinkled in disgust as he leapt over something sticky. But he kept going, running deeper into the dark. Occasionally, other holes would open up to the side or above, the whole place a network of interlocking tunnels and dens. As they ran, they could hear the hyenas' eerie laughter bouncing through the tunnels. The hyenas' heads shot down from smaller openings above as they tried to grab the cubs, each time just barely missing them.

Coming around a corner, Simba and Nala skidded to a stop. Right in front of them was a baby hyena. For a long moment, cubs and hyena just looked at one another, not sure who was more surprised—the cubs stumbling on the baby hyena or the hyena baby getting unexpected visitors. The little hyena's eyes were wide as it cocked its head. Simba was just about to smile at the kind of cute little guy when, suddenly, the baby bared its teeth. Simba and Nala jumped back and screamed as they realized, cute or not, the baby wanted a snack, too.

Once more, they began to race through the tunnels, now with the baby hyena close behind. Simba's head swiveled side to side as he desperately searched for a way up and out of the maze of tunnels. But everywhere he looked, he was met with more dens. The hyenas' home was impossible to escape! Just as he was about to give up, he heard Nala shout. Looking ahead, he saw a beam of light. A way out!

With a burst of speed, he and Nala raced toward the light and shot out into the fading sun of late afternoon. Not stopping, they ran full speed away from the dens and toward the steep hill at the far side of the Elephant Graveyard. Behind them, they could hear the hyenas closing in.

Reaching the hill, Simba began to climb. But his paws couldn't get a grip on the steep and slick rock and he slid back down. Beside him, Nala's attempts were just as futile. They couldn't get out the same way they had come in! They were trapped.

Hearing the terrible—and now frighteningly close—sound of hyena laughter, Simba slowly turned around. Then he gulped. Not only were they trapped, but they were trapped and facing a whole pack of hungry hyenas.

CHAPTER SIX

Simba turned and looked over at Nala. His friend was shaking, her eyes wide with fear. He had never seen her so scared and it made him even more frightened. He took a deep breath. This was all his fault. He had gotten them into this mess. He had to be the one to get them out—or at least he had to try.

Stepping in front of Nala, he planted his paws and puffed up his chest. Then, tilting back his head, he roared. Or, rather, he *tried* to roar. But he was a cub and his roar was not very loud. It barely sounded over the hyenas' heavy breathing.

The hyenas began to laugh hysterically. Some grabbed their bellies and fell to the ground, while others just howled and howled. Kamari, the tougher and meaner of Shenzi's two minions, pointed at Simba and, still laughing, shouted, "Did you hear that—the future king?" Overcome with laughter, he fell to the ground.

"Our enemy!" Azizi said, also laughing. "I'm so scared. Do it again!"

Simba growled under his breath. They were making fun of him. Fine. They thought he was just a little lion cub with a silly roar. Well, he would show them. Opening his mouth, he once more let out a roar.

Only this time, the roar wasn't tiny. It was huge. It shook the ridge and every hyena to the core. Simba's mouth snapped shut as he realized exactly *who* had just roared.

Turning, he had only a moment to see his father standing on top of the ridge before the king roared again and charged. In a flash of red and gold, Mufasa raced down the steep side of the hill and right into the throng of hyenas. His teeth snapped and his claws flashed as he threw aside the hyenas, scattering the yipping beasts in a cloud of dust. Simba watched open-mouthed as his father single-handedly put the hyenas in their place. He had never seen anything like it.

As the other hyenas started to flee, Shenzi stepped forward. Her lips curled back, revealing her fangs as she tried to stare down Mufasa. But the king didn't flinch. Snarling, he lifted a paw, extended his claws, and swiped. The blow hit Shenzi right on the leg, sending her flying backward. She landed with a thud.

Mufasa stalked forward, sending Shenzi scrambling back until she was cornered against a wall.

There was no place to run.

Mufasa stared down at the queen of the hyenas, his eyes boring into her with hatred. "If you ever come near my son again . . ." he said threateningly.

Shenzi shook her head. "No, Mufasa," she said weakly. "Never. Never again."

"You've been warned, Shenzi," Mufasa said. Then he turned and looked at the remaining hyenas, clustered together. He didn't say anything, but he didn't need to. Immediately, they began to slink away, disappearing down their holes and into their caves. Shenzi was the last to go. Getting up, she kept her head down as she limped up the rocks and into her own cave.

As the dust settled, Mufasa turned and looked at Simba. Simba shrank down, his eyes filling with tears. "Dad—I'm . . . I'm sorry," he said softly.

In response, Mufasa turned his back on Simba. "Let's go home," he said, staring straight ahead.

Hanging his head, Simba began to follow his father

back toward the safety of the Pride Lands. Beside him, Nala tried to offer comfort, but he ignored her. He didn't deserve it. Not now. He had disappointed his father. And that scared him more than facing a pack of hyenas.

CHAPTER SEVEN

As they reached the Pride Lands, the sun was beginning its slow descent behind the horizon. The savannah was a riot of colors—golds, oranges, and reds hitting the grasses and making them appear to be on fire. Herds of animals were unhurriedly making their way home, eyes heavy and bellies full. It was usually Simba's favorite time of day.

Usually.

But not this evening. Glancing up from beneath lowered lashes, Simba looked at his father. Mufasa's back was still tense, his steps still angry. In the time they had been walking from the Elephant Graveyard, his anger had ceased to subside. Simba opened his mouth to apologize but shut it again. What good would it do? He had betrayed his father's trust. There was no apology great enough.

"Zazu, take Nala back to Pride Rock."

Simba's head snapped up at the sound of his father's voice. The king had come to a stop, his eyes fixed on a point in the distance. He didn't even look at Zazu as he spoke. Nervously, Simba glanced over at Nala. She shrugged, not sure what was going on, either.

Zazu nodded. "Yes, sire," he said. He paused before adding, "Should I take Simba?"

"No," Mufasa answered. "I have to teach my son a lesson."

Simba gulped. To his surprise, Zazu came to his defense. "Sire, don't be too hard on him," the majordomo urged. "I remember a cub—a certain headstrong cub—who was always getting into scrapes. And he achieved some prominence—did he not?"

For the first time since leaving the hyenas, Simba thought he saw a flash of light in his father's eyes. "You've known me too long, Zazu," he said, his voice gentler than before. Turning, he looked over at Simba. "Come here," he commanded.

In response, Simba crouched down into the grass. He didn't know why he did it. It wasn't like his father couldn't see him. He hadn't become invisible, and while the grass was not bright green, it was not yet the weathered brown that might have offered him at least a little camouflage. Still, he lay there, his head on his paws, his eyes down, even as Zazu and Nala left and it grew silent.

"Simba!"

His father's voice broke the silence. Nervously, Simba inched forward in the grass. When his father called his name again, Simba reluctantly got up and began to walk toward his father. He was almost there when he stumbled. Looking down to see why, he saw his own paw inside the deep impression left by his father's. The king's print dwarfed Simba's as did his shadow, which suddenly loomed over him.

Craning his head up, Simba saw his father looking down at him. Mufasa's gleaming mane glowed even redder in the fading sunlight and cast crimson shadows over his muscled body. His deep brown eyes stared into Simba's. Finally, he spoke. "You deliberately disobeyed me," he said. His tone was even, emotionless.

"I know," Simba said.

Suddenly, as if a switch had been flipped on, emotion flooded through the king. "You could have been killed!" he shouted, his voice shaking. "And what's worse—you put Nala in danger!" Tears welled up in Simba's eyes as Mufasa continued. "Do you understand what's at stake? You jeopardized the future of our pride!"

Tears poured down Simba's cheeks. He had never meant to endanger the pride or hurt Nala. He had never meant to hurt anyone. "I just wanted to show you I could do it!" he said, his voice sounding tiny even to his own ears. "That I could be brave like you."

For a long moment, Mufasa didn't say anything, and the pit in Simba's stomach grew. Having his father angry was one thing. But if he wouldn't talk to him? That would be the worst punishment possible. His father was his world. He was Simba's everything. Not being able to hear his voice would kill him. Just as Simba was about to beg him to say something, Mufasa finally spoke. "I'm only brave when I have to be, Simba," he said. "When there's no other choice."

Simba cocked his head. *When there's no other choice?* He repeated the words silently. No other choice? But his father was always brave. "You're not scared of anything," Simba pointed out.

Mufasa shook his head. "I was today," he said, his voice growing softer.

"You *were*?" Simba said, amazed.

"Yes," Mufasa said. "I thought I might lose you."

Simba's stomach began to unclench as he realized that his father's anger had not been caused by disappointment. Mufasa was angry because he loved him. A small smile tugged at Simba's lips. "Oh," he said. "I guess even kings get scared, huh?"

"More than you could ever know," Mufasa said, mirroring his son's smile.

"But you know what?" Simba said. "I think those hyenas were even scared-er." As Mufasa let out a deep laugh, the knot in Simba's stomach disappeared and the weight he had been carrying on his shoulders vanished. Letting out the breath he'd been holding, Simba finally started laughing, too. He had messed up, big-time. But it was going to be okay. He and his dad would be okay.

"That's 'cause nobody messes with your dad!" Mufasa said, still laughing. Then, lifting a paw, he gestured for Simba to come closer. Mufasa pulled him into a hug, and father and son embraced for a long moment, each lost in thoughts of how close they had come to not being able to share any more moments like this one. Then, letting out a playful growl, Simba reached up and grabbed Mufasa's mane.

CHAPTER SEVEN

As the pair rolled around on the warm grass, the sun finally sank beneath the horizon and the first of the night's stars began to emerge in the sky. Father's and son's laughter mingled with the last of the birdcalls and a loan elephant trumpeted good night. Finally, tumbling to a stop, Simba landed on top of his father's massive chest.

Mufasa's chest rose and fell, lifting Simba up and down in a rhythmic sway, lulling him and comforting him. All the earlier fear and sadness faded as he and his father silently lay there, enjoying each other's company. Simba's paw curled and uncurled in his father's thick mane and he sighed happily. "Dad," he said softly, lifting his head up, "we're pals, right?"

"Right," Mufasa said with a nod, the deep rumble of his voice shaking Simba.

"And we'll always be together, right?"

To Simba's surprise, his father didn't answer right away. His mouth turned down, not in anger, but in thought. He sighed. Finally, he turned his head so he could look Simba in the eyes as he spoke. "Simba," he said seriously. "Let me tell you something my father told me: 'Look at the stars.'"

Flipping over onto his back, still on his father's chest, Simba looked up. The stars filled the sky, creating a sparkling blanket. In contrast, the savannah looked even darker, cast in deep shadows but seemingly still. But Simba knew hidden among the tall grasses and up in the high trees, animals that came out at night lay and lurked.

"The great kings of the past look down on us from those stars," Mufasa said, his eyes trained on the sky.

Simba looked up, straining to see the kings in the stars. But all he saw were twinkling lights and the moon. No kings. "Really?" he asked uncertainly.

"Yes," Mufasa said. "So, whenever you feel alone, just remember that those kings will always be up there to guide you." He paused before adding, "And so will I."

"But I can't see them, Dad," Simba said softly. *And so will I.* Why had his dad said that? Mufasa's voice had sounded so sad that Simba felt suddenly sad himself, like there was something he didn't know that his father did.

His father gave him a gentle nudge with his nose. "Keep looking, Son," he said. "Keep looking."

Together, father and son lifted their heads and looked up to the sky. Simba wasn't sure what his father was talking about—and he still only saw stars—but it didn't matter. He trusted his dad. And, more importantly, he loved his dad. And the reason they were lying under the stars together didn't matter. What mattered was that they were together. And they would be together forever.

CHAPTER EIGHT

Shenzi was angry. How dare Mufasa just storm in and act like she should bow to him! It was *his* son who had trespassed to begin with. As queen, she had every right to punish the young cub as she saw fit—even if that meant making him a snack. And yet, here she was, licking a new wound on *her* leg while Mufasa and Simba pranced back to the Pride Lands. Her eyes narrowed as she gave her leg an angry lick. It just wasn't right.

Shenzi lifted her eyes to look around her lair. The cave was the largest of all the dens and offered room for at least half a dozen hyenas. She usually had visitors at any given time, and that number always included Kamari and Azizi, her main minions. The pair were currently sitting on the floor below the ledge Shenzi reclined on, snapping at each other and complaining. She half-listened, their words becoming white noise as she went back to taking care of her wound. Kamari and Azizi were strong hunters, but neither was particularly bright, and Shenzi had learned long ago it was better to ignore them than engage with them.

"Next time Mufasa comes here," Kamari said, "I'm going to teach him a lesson he'll never forget."

Azizi cocked his head. "Come on, Kamari. What could *you* possibly teach him? He's a king—very wise," he said, once again completely missing the mark.

Kamari let out a sigh. "I wasn't actually going to teach him anything," he said.

Still not getting what his friend meant, Azizi

smiled. "You could teach him how we chase the sick and injured," he suggested helpfully.

"What I meant was," Kamari said, his words clipped and his claws digging into the dirt as he tried not to scream in frustration, "he will pay for what he's done to us."

Azizi's eyes widened in comprehension and he began to nod. Then he smiled widely and let out a happy little cackle. "Then you're in luck! Because there he is!"

Shenzi's head snapped up and her hackles rose. Following Azizi's gaze, she saw the faint outline of a lion moving toward them through the darkness of the cave entrance. Slowly, Shenzi got to her feet and began to make her way toward the opening. The sun outside somehow made the cave seem even darker, and the shadow of the lion took shape as he came closer. Shenzi's eyes narrowed and her lips pulled back. The lion walked slowly and casually, as if he didn't have a care in the world that he was walking into a den full of hungry, angry hyenas.

Shenzi began to shake her head. She knew Mufasa. This lion wasn't him. There was something slinky in the way he moved, his head down and the mane thin. Mufasa's walk was commanding; his head was always high. Behind the lion, hyenas began to emerge from their dens, their teeth bared, growling and hissing as they began to surround him.

Finally, the lion walked out of the shadows. Shenzi raised an eyebrow. As she had suspected, it was not Mufasa. Instead, it was his brother, Scar. She cocked her head, keeping her distance as she waited to see what he had to say. But she wasn't a fool. She signaled to the hyenas to be ready. If he made a move toward her, he would become the snack Simba should have been.

"You fools have stripped your land of every living thing," Scar began, looking around at the dark cave full of the remains of earlier meals. "And yet, I send two little cubs your way—and they come back alive."

Kamari shrugged. "I guess we'll have to eat you instead."

Scar didn't even flinch. "Why eat one meal—when you can be feasting the rest of your lives?"

The moment Scar had started to speak, Shenzi had been irritated. He was no better than his brother—coming in and making fun of their home and mocking their abilities to hunt. But a feast for the rest of their lives? That had her intrigued. "What could you possibly offer us?" she asked suspiciously.

Turning, Scar met her gaze and nodded. "A place where you can fill your bellies," he answered. "Where everything the light touches is yours for the kill."

Shenzi let out a laugh. So that was what he was offering? "The Pride Lands are not yours to give," she pointed out. "The king controls those hunting grounds." And they all knew Mufasa was not to be messed with—that his lands were off-limits to their kind.

"That's why we're going to kill him."

The laughter died in Shenzi's throat. Beside her, Kamari and Azizi murmured nervously. "Do not take me for a fool," she finally said. "Lions and hyenas have fought since the beginning of time. You would never take our side!"

Scar shrugged, not quick to argue. "My kind may hate you," he said in agreement. "But I see greed as a virtue. I call it ambition. When I am king, the mighty will be free to take whatever they want."

Shaking her head, Shenzi turned and walked back to her ledge. Scar might have grand plans and dreams of being a king, but Mufasa was too powerful. They could never challenge him. They may have him beat in terms of numbers, but he had the lionesses. The hyenas would never make it to the Pride Lands before they were attacked and turned back. Scar was foolish to even think of taking down his brother. Over her shoulder, she said just that.

"My brother has something he never had before," Scar responded. "A weakness. Something that clouds his judgment . . ."

Shenzi stopped, the pain in her leg throbbing. She looked down at the fresh wound. Scar was right.

Mufasa *did* have a weakness, something that made him act impulsively and put himself in danger unnecessarily. "Simba," she said, turning around and making her way closer to Scar.

He nodded. "Indeed."

A slow smile spread over Shenzi's face. Perhaps Scar wasn't that crazy after all. Perhaps there *was* a way to get the Pride Lands—and never go hungry again. "What do you need from us?" she asked as the hyenas around her yipped in agreement.

"Just one thing," Scar answered, his own evil smile mirroring hers. "Be prepared."

Simba yawned. He and his dad had not gotten home until late, and by the time he'd had a quick bath and gotten something to eat, he had barely been able to keep his eyes open. He'd fallen asleep before his head hit his paws and the morning had arrived far too quickly.

Now he lay in the sunshine, away from the other cubs, listening to the murmurs of his mother and the other lionesses as they talked quietly. Simba heard his name and his ears perked up as he tried to make out what the female lions were saying. He got only bits and pieces, but it was enough to know Sarabi had filled them in on his Elephant Graveyard adventure.

Feeling a few of the lionesses' eyes focused on him, Simba got to his feet and made his way down the rocks toward the flat ground below. He could rest there for a bit, without the judgmental glances to make him feel even worse than he already did. But to his surprise, he ran into his uncle. Scar was standing outside his cave, as though he had been waiting for Simba. Catching his nephew's eye, he gestured for Simba to follow.

Now Simba found himself walking along the floor of the deep canyon that cut through the heart of the Pride Lands. Beside him, Scar slunk along, his lean body the same tan color as the canyon walls. Simba wasn't sure why his uncle had come to him—until Scar said, "I heard you had quite the adventure yesterday."

As he spoke, he turned and looked down at Simba. Simba's shoulders sank. Apparently, it wasn't just the lionesses who knew. Even his uncle had heard about the run-in with the hyenas.

Simba nodded. "My dad was pretty upset with me," he said. *Actually, he was furious with me,* Simba added silently. *But I don't need to tell Scar that. Unless he already knows. Which he probably does.* Not for the first time, Simba wished the network of the Pride Lands wasn't quite so quick to spread news. It was hard to do anything without everyone knowing. He felt bad enough that he had disappointed his father, but in a way, he felt as though he had disappointed the animals of the Pride Lands, too.

But to his surprise, Scar didn't say anything about what had happened. Instead, he offered a way to make things better. "I think I know a way for you to make it up to him," he said as they continued to walk through the canyon. High above, birds flew through the air, small dots on the breeze. Gusts of sand billowed over the ridge, an indication of a passing animal. Otherwise, it was peaceful. Simba looked up at his uncle curiously. What did he mean? As if reading his thoughts, Scar continued. "A gift that will make him forget it ever happened."

Simba cocked his head. "But he's the king," he pointed out. "What could *I* give *him*?"

"Your roar," Scar replied without hesitation.

"My roar?" Simba repeated.

Scar nodded. Then, to prove his point, he jumped at a small tree, startling a few birds. As they flew into the sky, their squawks bounced off the walls of the canyon, making it sound as if there were hundreds, not a mere dozen of them. Scar looked over at Simba. "Did you hear that?" he said. "This gorge is where all the lions come to find their roar."

Simba's eyes grew wide. Find his roar? That sounded amazing. He had a flash of the weak attempt he had made back at the Elephant Graveyard. It had truly been pitiful. If he could make his roar bigger, it *would* go a long way toward impressing his dad. But then his eyes narrowed. He had never heard of lions coming to the gorge to practice their roars before. "All lions?" Simba asked. "Even my dad?"

"Even Mufasa," Scar said. "He came here when he was your age—refused to leave until his roar could be heard above the rim!"

Simba craned his head and looked all the way up at the ridge, high, high above. The birds Scar had startled were still flying to reach it. "All the way up there?" he asked. It seemed impossible.

But Scar apparently disagreed. "That's when you know you've found it," he said. "With a little practice, you'll *never* be called a cub again."

Never be called a cub again. That *would* be a great gift to give his dad. If he could show him that he had learned his lesson *and* found his own roar, Mufasa would have to be proud of him. Excited, he began to bounce up and down on his paws. He was going to do this! "Here I go!" he shouted. "Watch this!" Taking a deep breath, he rushed forward and then stopped short. Raising his head, he let out a roar. The small sound bounced off the canyon walls once, twice, and then stopped. Simba's excitement faded slightly at his first failed attempt.

"You'll get it, Simba," Scar said, giving him an encouraging nudge. "It just takes time. I'll check on you later."

As his uncle turned to go, Simba called after him. "Dad will be so proud, won't he?"

Scar stopped and looked over his shoulder. "It's a gift he'll never forget," he said. Then, with another wave good-bye, he turned once more and began to walk away.

Simba watched him go. There had been something odd in the way his uncle looked at him that made his tummy feel funny. Almost like Scar knew something Simba didn't. Then Simba shrugged. It was probably nothing. After all, he had barely spent any time with his uncle. He didn't know him well enough to know if he was acting funny. And Scar *had* given him a great idea for a gift.

CHAPTER EIGHT

Stalking over to the tree now empty of birds, Simba spotted a small chameleon, its scaly skin not quite the same color as the tree it was trying to hide on. Creeping closer, with his belly nearly touching the ground, he kept his eyes on the chameleon. Inch by inch, he moved until his paws touched the top of one of the tree's roots. Then he lifted his head and let out a roar.

The chameleon didn't react. He just kept walking on his way.

Simba's eyes narrowed. So the chameleon wasn't scared. Well, he would show him what a real lion sounded like. Once more, he took a deep breath, and then, with all the strength his body could muster—he roared.

The sound echoed up and around the walls of the gorge, bouncing between the flat surfaces of the rust-colored rocks. Simba smiled as he watched the chameleon stop in his tracks and heard his own roar echoing back to him. "See?" Simba said proudly. "That scared you!" He roared again.

This time, the chameleon turned a startling shade of green and ran down the tree, ducking under a rock at the base of the trunk. Watching him, Simba felt a sudden sense of unease. His roar hadn't been *that* big. The chameleon shouldn't have been scared back to its original color. Unless . . .

Suddenly, he realized that he could no longer hear his own roar bouncing between the canyon walls. It had been drowned out by something much louder. Something that sounded like thunder, only louder than any thunder he had ever heard before. Simba lifted his head to see if storm clouds were on the horizon, and his eyes grew wide. The sky at the top of the gorge had grown dark. But not from clouds.

A herd of wildebeests had appeared at the top of the ridge. As Simba watched, hundreds of the heavy animals spilled over the ridge and began to wildly gallop down into the gorge. Big and small alike, the wildebeests careened out of control, their bellows drowned out by the sound of their own pounding hooves. From where Simba stood, it looked as if they had become one single giant mass. A giant mass of dust and noise and deadly hooves—all coming right toward him.

Simba turned—and ran for his life.

CHAPTER NINE

Mufasa stood still, his eyes scanning the horizon. His patrol had been quiet so far. An angry elephant and a dispute between two meerkat families over feeding grounds had kept him occupied for a short time. Otherwise, the savannah had been peaceful, and Mufasa had found himself taking the time to enjoy the sun on his coat and the quiet that was such a rarity for him. He smiled as his mind wandered to thoughts of Simba. His son had been so upset after his run-in with the hyenas, as had Mufasa. But that night, as he'd shown his son the same patterns in the sky that his own father had shown him years ago, any lingering bad feelings faded.

Suddenly, as he sensed movement in the distance, Mufasa's head snapped up. The smile vanished and his eyes narrowed as he saw a cloud of dust rising from the canyon that cut through the center of the Pride Lands.

The telltale flapping of wings alerted Mufasa to the arrival of Zazu. He knew, even before his majordomo spoke, what he was going to say. Nevertheless, he allowed him to report.

"Sire," Zazu said. "The herd is on the move."

Mufasa nodded. "I know . . ." he answered. But it was strange. The herd had only just moved to their summer feeding grounds a few days ago. It was unlikely they would be turning back already. Unless . . .

As if on cue, Scar burst through the thick grass, running straight toward them at his fastest speed. Skidding to a stop, he gulped in deep breaths, his eyes panicked. "Mufasa!" he cried. "Quick! Stampede! In the gorge." He paused. It was only a moment, but in that moment, Mufasa felt his heart stop. For there was something in his brother's eyes that sent fear through him like a spear. And then, Scar spoke. "Simba's down there!"

"Simba?" Mufasa repeated, the fear solidifying.

Not waiting for confirmation, Mufasa turned and took off in the direction of the gorge. Above him, Zazu's wide wings flapped wildly as he, too, set off to find Simba. They had to get to him—before it was too late.

Simba ran. He ran as fast as he could. But it wasn't fast enough. As a full-grown lion he might have stood a chance of getting out of the way of a herd of charging wildebeests, but he wasn't fully grown. He was just a cub. Just a cub with a tiny roar and an uncanny ability to get in trouble.

His little paws flew over the shaking ground as

he rounded a curve in the canyon. Dust clouded the air and all he could hear was the sound of the wildebeests growing closer and closer. As one rocketed by, narrowly missing him, Simba spotted a tree branch overhead. The branch was dead, long since removed from whatever tree it had belonged to, but in that moment, it was an escape. With one final burst of energy, Simba leapt onto it, scurrying up and holding on for dear life.

Below him, the dust grew thicker as the herd thundered below the branch. With each wildebeest that passed, the branch shook, causing Simba to cry out. *How am I ever going to get out of this?* he thought as he clung desperately to the little safety he had. If he made it out of this mess, he was never going to leave Pride Rock ever again.

Suddenly, through the dust, Simba saw a flash of color. Dull at first, the color grew more vibrant until, with a whoosh, Zazu emerged out of the dust. "ZAZU!" Simba screamed.

"HOLD ON!" Zazu shouted back.

Do I have a choice? Simba almost retorted. But he stopped. Zazu was there to help. If he told Simba to hold on, Simba was going to do just that. Keeping his eyes on Zazu's brightly colored beak, he watched the bird flap up toward the ridge nearby. He let out a happy cry as he spotted his father and Scar standing together. *Scar must have told Dad I was here,* Simba thought. It didn't matter that his surprise gift was no longer a surprise. His dad was there. He would save him. Just like he always did.

But Mufasa wasn't moving. The giant lion was staring down at the sides of the steep canyon. Following his gaze, Simba gulped. It was a sheer drop from where they stood. Mufasa would have to go all the way back to the entrance of the gorge if he was going to make it down. And by the time he did that, Simba's tree branch—and Simba himself—would probably be smashed to smithereens.

Watching anxiously, Simba saw his father back up, disappearing from sight. Then, suddenly, he reappeared, racing toward the ridge. He leapt—his body arcing high and long over a narrow spot in the gorge. He landed with a thud on the other side, and without breaking his stride, he began to race down the rocky side. While the opposite wall was sheer, the one Mufasa made his way down now offered some outcroppings. Still, the momentum of his jump and his body was strong. Reaching the bottom, he kept going, racing toward the middle of the canyon floor and Simba beyond.

As Simba's branch creaked ominously, Mufasa jumped up on a small plateau of rock opposite his son. "I'm coming, Simba!" he shouted, his deep voice loud even over the sound of the stampeding wildebeests.

Looking down at the sea of brown-and-black bodies, Mufasa's eyes narrowed. Simba had seen that look before. His father was making a plan. Sure enough, a moment later he leapt off the plateau—and straight into the middle of the running herd. Battling his way against the sea of animals, he kept going, trying to reach his son.

Up on the ridge, Zazu watched in terror as the king desperately tried to get to Simba. But the herd was out of control. And huge. If they didn't stop running, Mufasa—and Simba—would never get out of there alive. Flapping his wings wildly, he looked down at Mufasa and then back over his shoulder at Pride Rock, then frantically back at Mufasa.

"I'll help them, Zazu!" Scar said. "You get the pride! GO!"

Zazu turned, surprised. He had nearly forgotten the other lion was still there. He didn't trust Scar one bit. But he could use the lionesses' help to turn the wildebeests back. With a nod, he turned and began to fly toward Pride Rock.

Behind him, Scar watched him go, a sneer slowly spreading across his face. *Yes, fly away, little birdie,* he thought. *Fly far, far away. I'll take care of Mufasa.* His smile grew wider. His plan was working out brilliantly. The hyenas had played their part—scaring the wildebeests into a stampede—and Simba had been wonderfully naïve. Yes, he would certainly take care of Mufasa. And then he would help himself—to everything that had belonged to the king.

Almost at the tree, Mufasa let out a roar of pain as he was once again struck on the side by a wayward wildebeest. He could see the fear in his son's eyes and could make out the growing crack in the branch. He *had* to get to him. They were running out of time. But for every step he took, a wildebeest pushed him back two and he was growing weaker by the moment.

Pushing through the pain, Mufasa bowed his head and, using it like a battering ram, knocked aside a pair of wildebeests in his way. He was now only a few feet from his son. But to his horror, as he watched, a wildebeest crashed right into the branch. Simba was thrown free, his body tumbling head over tail up into the air. Then he began to fall, straight down toward the herd.

Without hesitation, Mufasa sprang into the air, his jaws gaping wide. Snatching Simba right out of the air, he held him gently—but firmly—in his mouth and began to run. For a few wonderful moments, Mufasa felt his heartbeat slow ever so slightly. He had his son. They were going to be okay.

And then another wildebeest slammed into him.

As the air was knocked from Mufas's lungs, Simba was knocked from his mouth. The cub hit the ground and began to roll, narrowly avoiding being trampled by a dozen hooves. Pain ricocheted through Mufasa's side; he shook his head and began to make his way over to Simba. Once more, he grabbed him and then, spotting a small, stable ledge, he threw him onto it. Simba would be safe there for now. But the ledge was too small for both of them. He would need to find another place to wait it out until the stampede was over. "Don't move, Son!" he shouted.

Simba nodded and opened his mouth to speak, but before he could, another wildebeest knocked into Mufasa. Distracted as he was by Simba, the blow caught Mufasa off guard and he fell back, disappearing into the sea of wildebeests.

Mufasa saw flashes of blue and then brown as

he was tossed and thrown head over feet. The thundering hoofbeats nearly deafened him and he could barely breathe, the air was so thick with dust. But then he heard a single word. "DAD!" Simba's cry broke through all the other noise, giving him one last burst of strength.

Pushing himself up, up, up toward the thin line of blue sky he could see, Mufasa burst out of the herd and onto the rough, rocky side of the gorge. Wounded and bleeding, he clung to the rocks. His breath came in gasps and for a moment, he just hung there, not sure he could make it to the top. But out of the corner of his eye, he spotted Simba, watching. He *had* to keep going. Inch by painstaking inch, he began to climb. His legs shook and his vision blurred, but still he climbed until, finally, he felt a breeze ruffle his mane. He had reached the top. His back legs scrabbled at the side of the cliff, trying to find leverage.

Hearing footsteps as he clung to the top of the ledge, he lifted his gaze and found a familiar pair of eyes staring down at him from the safety of the top. "Scar!" he shouted. "Brother! Help me . . ."

But to his surprise, Scar didn't move. Instead, he just stared down at Mufasa, as though he were looking at a stranger, not his own flesh and blood. Groaning, Mufasa pulled himself still farther up, hooking his paws over the edge.

Finally, Scar moved. Only he didn't move to help him. Instead, the lion reached out and dug his own claws right into the tops of Mufasa's paws. Mufasa let out a cry of surprise and pain.

"Long live the king," Scar hissed. And then, as if he were swatting a fly, Scar swiped Mufasa across the face and knocked him backward—down, down, down—into the dust and thunder of the charging herd.

CHAPTER TEN

"DAD!"

Simba's eyes followed his father as he fell from atop the ridge. For one happy moment Simba had thought Mufasa made it safely to the top. He had watched as his father clung to the lip of the ridge, the muscles in his back legs visible even from all the way down in the gorge as he struggled to push himself to safety. Simba's breath had caught in his throat and he had started to cheer.

But the cheer had turned to a scream as he watched his father fall backward and plunge toward the ground. Simba's gaze stayed on him as he fell toward the huge dust cloud created by the wildly stampeding wildebeests. He kept looking even as his father disappeared into the dust without a sound. One minute there—the next gone. And his gaze stayed trained on that very spot as the wildebeests' number began to dwindle and the stampede came to an end.

When the sound of the wildebeests' pounding hoofbeats could no longer be heard, Simba jumped off the rock and raced into the gorge toward the spot where he had seen his father fall. But while the herd was no longer there, the dust still was, making it hard to see. Simba frantically searched, mistaking rocks and mounds of dirt for his dad. Over and over again, he called out "Dad!"—but the only sound that came back was his own voice, echoing off the canyon walls.

Suddenly, finally hearing something other than his own voice, Simba looked behind him hopefully. "Dad?" he called out. But as the dust cleared, he saw it was just a lone wildebeest chasing after the herd. As the animal ran by him, Simba didn't even bother to look at it. He couldn't. Because all he could see was his father lying on the gorge floor beyond.

As a cry caught in his throat, Simba ran toward his father. "Dad!" he shouted, reaching his side. "It's okay! It's going to be okay!" But his father didn't move. His eyes stayed closed. His wide ribs did not rise and fall. Slowly, Simba reached out a paw and gently pushed against his father's side. "Come on—wake up! We gotta go home. . . ."

Tears began to fall. Simba scrunched his eyes closed and shook his head, not wanting to believe it, hoping he could wake up from this terrible nightmare. But when he opened his eyes, his father was still lying there, motionless. A coldness began to creep over Simba, and despite the warmth of the sun on the canyon floor, he began to shake.

"Help!" he screamed. "Somebody help!"

But his pleas went unanswered. He was alone. Truly and utterly alone. Letting out a sob, he lay down next to his father, curling up into a ball and pushing against Mufasa's sides in a vain attempt to seek some warmth from his father's body. The tears pooled under his cheeks as his paw clenched and unclenched around the great lion's mane in a motion that had become habit. He thought back to long nights tucked between his mother and father, of the warmth and comfort he had taken from feeling their steady breaths, his father's mane covering him like a blanket. His tears fell harder and harder, mixing with the dust in the air and making Simba cough.

Sitting up, his eyes grew wide. There, emerging from the dust, was his uncle. Hope flared in his tiny chest. Scar would know what to do. He would be able to fix his father. Leaping to his feet, Simba raced over. "Scar!" he shouted with a sob. "Help him! Please—" He tried to hug his uncle, but to his surprise, the older lion pulled back, a look of horror in his eyes.

"Simba," he whispered, looking at Mufasa. "What have you done?"

Simba backed away. What was Scar talking about?

He hadn't *done* anything. "It was a stampede," he said. "He tried to save me—it was an accident. I didn't mean for it to . . ." His voice trailed off, doubt creeping in. It wasn't his fault, was it? The stampede had just happened. And his dad was just trying to save him. There wasn't anything he could have done differently. . . .

As if sensing his doubt, Scar put a paw on Simba's shoulder. "Of course you didn't. No one means for these things to happen," he said gently. Simba looked up, startled to see the iciness in his uncle's eyes. And then Scar's voice changed, growing cold, as well. "But the king *is* dead. And if it weren't for you—he'd still be alive."

Fresh tears began to fall as Scar spoke aloud all the horrible thoughts Simba had only just begun thinking. And worse still, Scar had said the one word Simba had not dared even think until that very moment. *Dead.* His father was dead.

"Your father had such hopes for you," Scar continued, seemingly unbothered by the young cub's tears. "He gave you so many chances! And this is how you repay him!"

"I didn't know . . ." Simba protested weakly.

Scar shook his head. "What will your mother think?" he said. "A son who causes his father's death. A boy who kills a king?"

Simba began to sob harder, his whole body shaking. His mother was going to be devastated. The whole pride would hate him. If what Scar said was true, he had killed his own father. No one would believe it was an accident. And even if they did, they would never forgive him. How could they, when Simba couldn't even imagine forgiving himself? Through the blur of his tears, Simba looked up at his uncle. "What am I going to do?" he asked softly.

"Run," Scar answered. "Run away, Simba. Run away . . . and never return."

For a long moment, Simba stood there, shocked by his uncle's suggestion. But then his eyes fell on his father's lifeless body. His uncle was right. He had to run. He couldn't return to Pride Rock. Not now—not ever. Not when he was the reason Mufasa was gone.

CHAPTER TEN

I'm sorry, Dad, Simba said, taking one last look at his father. *I'm so very sorry.*

And then, turning, he began to run.

Scar watched as his nephew raced away, and a slow smile spread across his face. *Well,* he thought, *that worked out after all.* When he had come up with the plan to get rid of Mufasa, he had anticipated ridding himself of the pesky cub and future heir, too. In fact, it was necessary to his grand plan. But getting Simba to exile himself from the Pride Lands would probably do the trick.

Hearing footsteps behind him, Scar looked over. Emerging from the dust was Shenzi, along with twenty or so members of her pack. She looked down at Mufasa's lifeless body and then up at Scar. She nodded, pleased to see that Scar was living up to his promise.

In the distance, Simba was growing smaller and smaller. Scar watched, the wheels spinning in his mind. True, it would work if Simba were to live in exile. But that left a few too many loose ends, in his opinion. And if there was one thing Scar didn't like, it was loose ends. No, it wouldn't do to let the little rug rat get away. He should take care of it—in a more *permanent* way.

Scar looked back at Shenzi and sneered. "Kill him," he said.

The hyenas didn't hesitate. Yipping and cackling, they took off after Simba. As they, too, disappeared in a cloud of dust, Scar nodded. Yes, he thought. That would be much better. No use risking Simba returning—now, or ever.

Simba ran. He ran and ran, trying to outrun his thoughts and the image of his father, lifeless on the gorge floor. But no matter how fast he went, he could see his dad, hear his uncle's accusations, imagine his mother's heartbreak. At the thought of his mother, Simba's steps slowed.

I shouldn't leave, he thought. *I need to be there for her. I should be the one to tell her. . . .*

Coming to a stop, he caught his breath. His father would not approve if he left now. That was not what Mufasa would have done. Simba was the king now. He had to act like one. With a sense of hope, Simba turned to head back. But as he did so, his eyes widened. Not even half a mile away, he could make out the telltale sounds of a pack of hyenas as they ran, kicking up a cloud of dust. A moment later he clearly heard their cackles, carried through the gorge, echoing eerily off its walls.

Simba let out a frightened cry and immediately turned to run once more. He needed to get out of there—now.

As he ran, the sides of the gorge began to narrow. Small holes appeared on either side, leading to tunnels that ran the length of the walls. Behind him, the hyenas' cries grew louder as they grew closer. Ducking into one of the small holes, Simba frantically began to claw his way up. The space was too small for the larger hyenas and he heard their frustrated cries as they were forced to turn and go around, continuing along until they found a bigger hole. Pushing their way into one such hole, they began to scramble over one another, desperate to snap their jaws around Simba's neck.

But luckily for Simba, the tunnels were all connected, and the combined weight of the hyenas was enough to send loose rocks sliding down, forming a natural ladder. Quickly, Simba began to race up toward the top of the ridge, bursting into the sunlight a moment later.

His triumph was short-lived, however. He had reached the top, but he had come up in a spot where there was nothing but a little bit of ridge and then a cliff that dropped straight down. There was nowhere to go.

A moment later, a huge hyena emerged behind him. His giant jaws snapped and drool dripped down, covering the rock in a slimy layer of saliva. He began to advance toward Simba. Simba looked back and forth between the hyena and the cliff, not sure which was the worse option. But just then, the hyena lunged.

Simba didn't hesitate. Letting out a cry, he threw himself off the cliff. Seconds later, the hyena followed, not by choice but because the momentum of his lunge had made it impossible for him to stop. Together, Simba and the hyena fell through the air. The ground had seemed so terribly far when Simba was up on the ridge, but as he helplessly dropped down, it approached far too rapidly. There was a thick canopy of trees below, and just visible through the clear patches, Simba could make out the hard ground.

The canopy grew closer and closer.

Simba closed his eyes as, beside him, the hyena kept snarling and snapping. Then he felt his body hit the leafy top of the canopy and he began to bounce from branch to branch, the sound of his body thudding against the wood loud, the pain excruciating. As if from a great distance, Simba could hear the sound of the hyena's pained screeches as he also fell through the trees. For what felt like forever, Simba dropped until finally, with a thunk, he landed hard on a wide branch. He reached out quickly to grip the sides of the wood, stopping his momentum and giving him the chance to hang on.

Letting out a deep breath, he lay there, trying to slow his pounding heart. He looked up, up, up to the ridge far above. He couldn't tell if there were any hyenas left but he had to imagine they assumed he was dead. He *should* have been dead. But somehow he wasn't. Getting to his feet, he walked across the branch to where it met the trunk of the tree. Driving his claws into the wood, he began to slowly make his way down to the ground in a series of slips and slides.

When he finally reached the bottom, he found the hyena lying motionless in the leaves. Simba didn't hesitate. Jumping over him, he began to run again. He wanted to put as much distance between himself and the ridge and those hyenas as possible. He had been foolish to think of going back. He could never return.

CHAPTER ELEVEN

Scar watched as the sun slowly inched over the distant horizon. As the beams touched the savannah, the grasses erupted in golds and oranges, as if on fire. It was a beautiful start to the day. A day he had been waiting for . . . for a long, long time.

Turning his back to the sunrise, Scar looked out over the gathered lions. They stared at him, suspicion in their eyes. A few of them were perceptive enough to look frightened, sensing that something wasn't right. His earlier arrival at the top of Pride Rock had been met with confusion. He never ventured above his den. Without saying a word to the other lionesses, he had made his way to Sarabi—and broken the news of Mufasa's death.

It had been a wonderful moment. Just as he had always imagined. Watching as Sarabi's eyes filled with understanding and then devastation, listening as the other lionesses lifted their heads and roared in grief. Through it all, Scar had stayed silent, waiting for his moment.

And now, the time had come. "Mufasa's death is a terrible tragedy," he began, addressing the pride. "The greatest leader the pride has ever known. To lose a brother—such a deep personal loss. And little Simba . . ." His voice trailed off as he pretended to be overcome with emotion. No, he *was* overcome—just not with sadness. When Shenzi had informed him that Simba had tumbled off the cliff, his plan had been made complete. What he felt now was simple—it was happiness. Or at least his version of happiness.

Taking a deep breath, Scar looked at Sarabi as he continued. "Simba—who had barely begun to live. A cub whose blood held our future." He shook his head. "It's almost too much to endure. I only wish I had gotten to the gorge in time—been there to save them." Turning his back on the lionesses, he began to walk toward the summit of Pride Rock. *Oh, I am good,* he thought as he hung his head and kept his steps slow and heavy, as though the burden of what he was about to do weighed on him. *Who wouldn't believe this performance? Mufasa might have gotten the muscles, but I got the acting chops.*

As he reached the top of the rock, he turned. Behind him the sun lifted completely above the horizon. "So, it is with a heavy heart that I must assume the throne," Scar went on, trying to keep his voice solemn. The lionesses began to murmur, and Scar saw Sarabi step forward, shaking her head. She could shake her head all she wanted. She had no choice. She would have to follow him. Unless . . .

"Mufasa and Simba are gone," he repeated. "Which means I am your king! But I must admit—I cannot bear this burden alone. After all, there is no king without his queen." He paused, waiting for Sarabi to acquiesce. To his annoyance, she snarled, shaking her head. He frowned but didn't push her. She would say yes. She would have to—after she saw what he had in mind. But until that time, he had one more trick up his sleeve. "And I will need some help to ensure the safety of the pride!"

Looking beyond the lionesses, Scar nodded. A moment later, Shenzi, followed by her pack, began to slink onto Pride Rock. The lionesses snarled, pushing their cubs behind them as the hyenas continued to creep up and over the rocks, invading every nook and cranny of the lions' home. "And so, from the ashes of this tragedy, we shall welcome the dawning of a new era," Scar announced. "A great and glorious future!"

Sarabi watched as the hyenas slowly surrounded her home. Their mangy, matted fur was dull and lifeless, and their evil cackles made her skin crawl. They didn't belong on Pride Rock. And as she lifted her head to look at Scar, she knew that neither did he. This was wrong. All of it was so wrong.

Mufasa was gone. Simba was gone. Her whole world was gone. And now, to make it worse, Scar was going to let the hyenas take over the Pride Lands. Signaling to the other lionesses, she turned and walked back into the den, her mind racing, her heart broken. She glanced at the spot where she and Mufasa and Simba had always slept, wanting nothing more than to lie down, close her eyes, and wake up from this terrible nightmare. But she knew that wouldn't happen. She would never again feel Mufasa's warmth next to her. She would never again hold Simba in her paws or hear his happy little laugh. He would never wake them up to see the sunrise or play hide-and-seek with Nala and the other cubs. Scar had been right about one thing—Simba's life had been ended too soon. He was supposed to be there, with her. And so was Mufasa.

Her heart heavy with grief, she turned and looked at the other lionesses. She could see the fear in their eyes and wanted to offer them comfort, but she could barely comfort herself. She was numb. She had been numb ever since Scar had stalked into the den and told her what had happened. He had acted as though he was upset, but Sarabi doubted it. There had been no love lost between the brothers. Sarabi had tried to get Mufasa to talk to her about why, but he had always changed the subject, pursuing topics like the weather or the state of the pride. She had never pressed the issue, but now she wished she had. It would be good to know more about Scar—now that he was their leader.

What are we going to do? she thought as a few of the youngest cubs, blissfully unaware of all that had happened, began to wrestle. *We can't let the hyenas take over. They'll destroy everything . . . they'll destroy* everyone.

"Sarabi?"

Looking down, Sarabi saw Nala standing in front of her. Tears filled the young cub's eyes, and Sarabi's heart broke anew. She realized she wasn't the only one to have lost Simba. Poor Nala had lost her best friend.

"Sarabi, what did Scar mean it is a 'new era'?" Nala asked. "Are the hyenas staying?"

Sighing, Sarabi lowered her head and rested it gently on Nala's. The movement, one that she had done hundreds of times with Simba, sent an ache through Sarabi. She inhaled deeply, taking in the scent of the den and the watering hole lingering on Nala's fur, the smell so close to Simba's. So close, yet so different.

Just like everything now.

"I honestly don't know, Nala," Sarabi finally said, lifting her head. She stood and walked back to the entrance of the den. Outside, the hyenas were helping themselves to the food from the lionesses' last hunt. She heard their nips and snarls as they fought one another for the few remaining bites. The lions never nipped or snarled. They killed what they needed and shared equally. "I think Scar believes we can live with the hyenas," she went on. "But lions and hyenas have never been able to live peacefully. . . ."

"Mufasa would never have let this happen," Nala said softly. "I miss him."

"I do, too, young one. I miss him so very much."

"What are we going to do?" Nala pressed. Behind her, a few of the older cubs had moved closer, interested to hear what Sarabi said.

Looking at their faces, Sarabi saw Simba in each. She couldn't let them down. She needed them to have something to believe in. It was what Mufasa would have wanted and what Simba would have deserved. Lifting her head, she gave a determined nod. "We," she said boldly, "are going to stay strong. We are not going to let the hyenas take over. That's what Scar wants, but it won't happen." She paused. She didn't trust Scar. She hadn't trusted the look in his eyes when he had told her Mufasa and Simba were gone. He had seemed almost eager to tell her. And then he had made the comment about her being his queen. She would *never* be his queen. Mufasa would remain in her heart for the rest of her life.

While his words might have sounded sincere and his declaration of a glorious future might have sounded promising, Sarabi knew better. The hyenas moving onto Pride Rock was just the beginning. Things would get worse. And it was her job, as the pride's queen, to keep calm and protect the lions—as best she could.

"I don't know what will happen," Sarabi finally said. "But I promise you, I will do my best to help us. Let the hyenas think they've won. Let Scar believe we will go along with his 'future.' But we will know that isn't the truth. We must keep our heads up, our ears open." She looked over at the older lionesses. "When he asks us to hunt, don't always succeed. Better we starve than feed those mangy hyenas. Never go anywhere alone. We need each other—the pride—now more than ever." The other lionesses began to murmur in agreement. Sarabi smiled gently at them. They had all suffered a loss. Yet they were still there, still strong. Looking once more out of the den, she gave another determined nod. "I promise you. Pride Rock will always be our home. . . ."

At least I hope so, she thought as she stared out at the cloudless blue sky, so strangely peaceful when inside she felt so stormy. *Because after all that I've lost today, I can't lose my home, too.*

CHAPTER TWELVE

Every bone in Simba's body hurt. His head pounded, and his eyes were swollen shut. The side of his body lying against the hard desert ground burned, as did the opposite side exposed to the sun.

He had been lying there for what felt like days. After his fall from the cliff, he had just turned and run blindly. His only goal: to get as far from the hyenas and the Pride Lands as possible.

So Simba had run. Soon the savannah grasses had given way to soft sand, which, in turn, had given way to an endless sea of brown dirt. The hard-packed ground, cracked from the unrelenting sun that beat down on it day after day, offered no protection for the young cub. He had gone without water or food, plodding forward slowly while his thoughts raced. Images of his father falling flashed through his mind. He saw Scar's look of dismay and horror. His head thundered with the sound of the wildebeests. And through it all, moving in and out of his other visions, he imagined his mother. He pictured her eyes full of tears as she heard about Mufasa's death and then imagined her anger when she realized he was the reason the king was gone. That thought alone was enough to keep Simba running. He could never return—not when he had let everyone down.

But now he was pretty sure returning wouldn't be an issue, since it seemed he would probably die out here. Over the pounding of his head and his own labored breathing he could make out the sound of buzzards flapping overhead. They always arrived when an animal was close to the end. The harbingers of death, as it were. The flapping came closer as the large birds descended, and then Simba heard a few of them land nearby. As they began to circle him, Simba tried to open his eyes, but the slightest movement sent pain screaming through his body and he finally gave up, letting his eyelids stay closed, blocking out the harsh sun and keeping him in the dark.

Then, suddenly, he heard the buzzards' wings begin to flap more frantically as they called out to each other. A moment later there was the unmistakable sound of hoofbeats and the ground under Simba shook. Just as a wave of exhaustion ushered him toward unconsciousness, Simba thought he heard a loud voice. The last thing he was aware of, before he slipped away, was someone shouting, "Bowling for buzzards!"

Pumbaa took a step back. The warthog liked to get a running start when he was bowling for buzzards.

Lowering his head, he let out a loud snort and waited for the birds to settle back down. It was far more fun to bowl if there were a lot of buzzards together. And if there was one thing Pumbaa liked, it was fun.

In fact, both he and his best friend, Timon, loved fun more than just about anything. It was why they were such good friends even though he was a warthog and Timon was a meerkat. And, as Timon liked to point out, Pumbaa was the brawn while Timon was the brains. But despite the differences, they were best pals.

Seeing that the time was right, Pumbaa pawed at the ground and once more charged at the buzzards. As he slammed into a handful, dust and feathers flew into the air, along with the remaining birds. Pumbaa let out another happy shout. "To think I woke up today with nothing to do," he said. "And look at what I've accomplished."

Timon, who had been hiding on Pumbaa's back to avoid the flying feathers and any unnecessary dirt, popped up. His big eyes, outlined with black, shifted nervously back and forth. He was always on the lookout for danger. That was the thing with meerkats. Unless they were safely underground, they were highly nervous creatures. And Timon was more nervous than most.

He was also hungrier than most meerkats. Food was always on his mind. "Are there any eggs?" he asked eagerly, looking over at where a few of the birds were still lying in a state of shock. "Please tell me there's an egg! If you scare 'em just right, the eggs come flying out."

Pumbaa shook his head. "No eggs this time." But then he paused, cocking his head. Just beyond the buzzards, he saw something. He hadn't noticed it before, being busy with buzzard bowling and all, but now he squinted his eyes, trying to make out what it was. Finally, he figured it out. "Look, Timon," he said. "There's a little yellow hair ball."

"I've always wanted a hair ball," Timon said, eagerly clapping his hands together. Urging Pumbaa closer, Timon looked down at the hair ball. "And it's just my size!"

As they stared down at the hair ball, Pumbaa's

eyes narrowed. There was something . . . different . . . about it. He couldn't quite put a finger on it. And then he figured it out. "Wait a second," he said. "This hair ball has four legs and a tail."

Timon shrugged. "I don't care," he said. "I'm a naked meerkat. The nights are chilly. That fur is mine!"

"Timon—I think it's alive," Pumbaa said, keeping his eyes trained on the hair ball. It did, in fact, appear that the hair ball was breathing.

Shaking his head, Timon jumped off Pumbaa's back and walked over to the hair ball. "Alive?" he repeated. "Why does everything have to be alive? Because if this hair ball is alive, it would be a—" Leaning down, Timon lifted the hair ball's paw. Then he let out a scream. "LION! Run for your life, Pumbaa! RUN!" Quickly, he scrambled back up onto Pumbaa's back and lowered himself out of sight.

But Pumbaa didn't run. He didn't back away at all. Instead, he just moved closer. Lowering his head, he smiled. "Timon, it's just a little lion," he said, his voice going all soft and gushy. "And he's so cute—"

Timon climbed down and narrowed his eyes. "Oh, yes, he's just adorable," he said, his voice full of sarcasm. "A five-hundred-pound monster who will drink my blood. We can call him"—he paused for dramatic effect—"PLEASE DON'T EAT ME!"

Ignoring his friend, Pumbaa continued looking down at the lion. Then he glanced around, narrowing his eyes. They were in the middle of the desert, miles from anywhere a lion would usually wander. There was not another creature, let alone a lion, in sight. "He's all alone," Pumbaa said sadly. But then his face brightened as a wonderful idea came to him. "Can we keep him? I promise to walk him every day! And clean up his little mess—"

Timon held up a finger, stopping Pumbaa mid-sentence. He had seen his friend get excited before. He had even let Pumbaa bring home a beetle once after the warthog begged and begged. But that hadn't ended well. And he doubted this would, either. "*You'll* be his little mess," he pointed out. "He'll eat you—then use me as a toothpick!"

"Some of my best friends are carnivores," Pumbaa pointed out. "And one day, when he's big and strong, he'll be on our side!"

"That's the stupidest thing I've ever heard," Timon retorted. "One day he'll be on *our* side." He began to laugh, his little belly heaving up and down. But suddenly, he stopped. His eyes widened. His nose twitched. Then he let out a shout. "I've got it!" he cried happily. "What if he's on *our* side?" he asked, repeating what Pumbaa had said only moments before as if it were a wholly original idea he had just come up with. "Ya know, having a ferocious lion around might not be such a bad idea."

Pumbaa began to hop around in glee. Ignoring the fact that Timon had completely hijacked his idea (or perhaps just oblivious), he looked happily down at the lion. "So, we can keep him?" he asked excitedly.

"Of course we're keeping the hair ball!" Timon answered. "Who's the brains of this operation?"

Just then, the lion's eyes fluttered open.

Timon let out a squeak and jumped onto Pumbaa.

He might be the brains, but he most definitely didn't want to be the wake-up snack. It would be safer to wait up there and see what happened. . . .

Simba heard voices. They sounded far away, like whoever was speaking was at the end of a long tunnel. A part of him wanted to keep his eyes closed in the hopes they would just go away and leave him alone. But another part, mostly the empty-stomach part, didn't agree.

Slowly, Simba opened his eyes. At first, all he could see was the blinding light of the sun and then spots as he snapped them shut again. He waited for the spots to fade, bouncing around like small stars in a dark sky. Finally, he tried again. This time, he opened his eyes slowly, allowing them to adjust to the light.

To his surprise, he found himself looking up at a meerkat and a warthog. They, in turn, were looking down at him. The meerkat seemed nervous, but the warthog looked thrilled to see him. Simba cocked his head. "Who . . . who are you?" he asked, his parched throat making the words sound scratchy.

"We're the guys who saved your life," the meerkat answered. "Risked everything—fought off angry vultures!"

"I'm Pumbaa," the warthog said, shooting his friend a look Simba couldn't quite read. "And this is Timon."

The meerkat nodded. "There were hundreds of them," he went on, clearly fixated on the vultures. "It was horrible. No need to thank us." He stopped and waited for the thanks he hadn't asked for. When Simba didn't say anything, Timon shrugged. "Did I mention we saved your life?"

Simba sighed. *Wish you hadn't,* he thought. *Would have saved everyone a lot of trouble.* Getting to his feet, he turned his back on Timon and Pumbaa and slowly began to walk away. Every step felt like he was walking over shards of glass and his stomach growled, his insides twisting in protest at the lack of food.

"Hey!" shouted Timon. "Where you going?"

"It doesn't matter," Simba answered as he continued

to walk. Seeing a small, dirty puddle of water, he lowered his head and took a few sips. The water was hot and full of grit but at least it curbed his thirst. All those times he had protested going all the way to the watering hole flashed through his mind. What he wouldn't give to have the chance to go there now. To be back with his mother, or playing with Nala. His shoulders slumped and he stopped drinking. What was the point of thinking about any of it?

Behind him, he heard Pumbaa's concerned voice. "He's so sad," the warthog said. "We have to help him, Timon!" Simba heard hoofbeats and then Pumbaa appeared next to him. "Hey, kid, what's eating ya?"

Before Simba could even answer, Timon piped up. "Nothing," he said. "He's the top of the food chain!" He paused and looked expectantly at the lion and the warthog. Both of them looked back blankly. "Get it?" he pressed. Nothing. "Food chain?" Still nothing. Shrugging, Timon moved on. "So, where ya from?"

"Who cares?" Simba snapped. "I can't go home." He was surprised by the defeat he heard in his own voice.

But it was the truth. What good would it do to tell Timon and Pumbaa about his old life? It was a life he could never get back.

Timon cocked his head. "So if you can't go home," he said, another thought coming to mind, "does that mean someone from home will come looking for you? And by someone, I mean a large hairy beast?"

"Nobody will ever look for me," Simba said softly.

To his surprise, Pumbaa seemed thrilled by that answer. "No family!" he cried. "So, you're an outcast!"

Timon was pleased, too. "That's great! So are we!" Clapping his hands, he gave Simba a huge smile. For the first time since Simba had opened his eyes, the meerkat seemed to relax. In fact, as Simba watched, Timon settled down on the ground near the muddy puddle and put his hands behind his head. "Tell us about it, kid. We love a good outcast story."

Pumbaa plopped himself down, too. "Those stories always make me cry," he said. "Especially if the outcast falls in a hole and has to eat his own foot."

Simba looked back and forth between the odd pair.

Were they serious? It was hard to tell. But even if they were, it wasn't like he was going to just tell them everything that had happened.

"Let me guess," Timon said. "You were too small?"

Simba shook his head.

"Too slow?" Timon asked.

Simba shook his head again.

"Anxious? Aggressive? Envious?"

Still, Simba just shook his head. But the meerkat's incessant questions had made him smile—slightly. For one brief moment, he almost felt like laughing. But then Pumbaa spoke, and the feeling vanished.

"I also like the ones when the outcast accidentally eats a relative," the warthog said, tears welling up in his eyes at the mere mention of it.

Simba's heart began to thud in his chest. Did they know somehow? Had word already gotten out from the Pride Lands about what he had done? Were they just trying to get him to admit it so they had confirmation that he was a killer? As Timon continued to list reasons why Simba might be an outcast, the young lion realized he was being paranoid. The pair didn't know anything. They were just being silly and guessing. But silly or not, they were reminding him of everything he had lost. Slowly, he began to back away. He didn't want to be there anymore.

"I did something terrible," he said, cutting Timon off. "I don't want to talk about it. Leave me alone."

Turning, he began to walk away. But the combination of the lack of food, his broken heart—which was still racing—and the hot sun was just too much for him. His vision grew blurry and then, with a thunk, he fell over onto the hard ground. He lay there, panting heavily as Timon and Pumba raced over.

"Kid!" Pumbaa said, sliding to a stop next to him. Worry was etched on his face as he looked down at Simba. He lowered his head and gently nudged Simba with the tip of one of his tusks. When Simba didn't move, Pumbaa once again lowered his head, only this time, Timon lent a hand, too, and together they got Simba back on his feet. Simba sighed deeply. "There must be something we can do?" Pumbaa pleaded, clearly not happy to see the lion cub so *un*happy.

Simba shook his head. The old him would have said thank you. He probably would have even had fun telling the warthog and the meerkat all about his crazy adventures and what kind of king he would be someday. But now all he could think about was what *had* happened. All he could see was his father's lifeless body, and all he could imagine was the look of disappointment on his mother's and Nala's faces. "Not unless you can change the past," he finally said.

"Nobody can change the past," Timon pointed out. "But the future—that's our specialty."

Despite himself, Simba looked up, intrigued. "You can change the future?" he asked.

Pumbaa nodded. "We'd be happy to change yours!" he exclaimed. "It's easy!"

Simba didn't understand. "How can you change something that hasn't happened?"

Thrilled to be asked a question he could answer—and sound smart doing so—Timon held up a finger. Always the showman, he waited for a long moment before answering. “Well, to change the future,” he said, “you gotta put the past behind you.” Taking his finger, he pointed it behind him.

“Way behind,” Pumbaa agreed. “I put mine behind that rock. Or was it that rock?” The warthog, distracted for a moment, began to sniff around a pile of rocks that all looked exactly the same.

Simba watched, a bemused expression beginning to spread over his face. Timon was ridiculous. There was no way to change the future, no matter what he said. And Pumbaa was just plain silly. Still . . . he couldn’t help listening as Timon went on. Forgetting his past? Being able to move on? It sounded better than where he was now, that was for sure.

“Look, kid,” Timon went on. “Bad things happen—and you can’t do anything about it, right?”

“Right,” Simba agreed.

To Simba’s surprise, Timon shook his head “Wrong!” he shouted. “When the world turns its back on you, you turn your back on the world!” His voice grew louder as he got caught up in the moment. Simba listened with growing interest as Timon and Pumbaa explained what he had to do as an outcast. They had a plan, he quickly learned, that included leaving the past behind him, embracing his future, and forgetting any wrongs.

When they paused, Simba narrowed his eyes. "That's not what I was taught," he said, thinking about the Circle of Life his father had described to him. How everything was connected, nothing was forgotten, and everything was important. It was the exact opposite of what Timon and Pumbaa were saying.

Timon shook his head. "Maybe," he suggested, "you need a new lesson. Repeat after me: *hakuna matata*."

"What?" Simba asked.

"It means no worries," Pumbaa explained, as though that made everything clearer.

Right. No worries, Simba thought as Pumbaa and Timon continued to ramble on. *That sounds fantastic. But how can anyone live without worries?*

Apparently, Timon and Pumbaa could. And they quickly told him just how. Their life, they informed him, hadn't always been so footloose and fancy-free. They hadn't always lived without worries. In fact, Pumbaa had spent his youth being the "stinky wart-hog" who'd had no friends—at least not any who would stand downwind.

As they continued to talk, Simba's mind began to race. They were right. He couldn't change the past. What had happened had happened. But maybe, just maybe, he could make his future better . . . even if it meant living out in the desert and not in the Pride Lands. He might never get to be king of the Pride Lands, but maybe he could become a master of not worrying.

CHAPTER THIRTEEN

Simba was still thinking about what his new future might be when Timon and Pumbaa finally stopped talking and realized he hadn't run away. And that it was time to head home. Jumping on Pumbaa's back, Timon gestured for Simba to follow.

Turning, the warthog began to trot off along a path only he seemed to see. Simba tried to keep up, but he was still tired and the ground was still hard, so he was slower than normal.

He nearly fell flat on his face several times before Pumbaa noticed he was lagging and stopped to let him catch up.

For the rest of the journey, Pumbaa kept to a slow trot. Simba, no longer forced to focus exclusively on staying upright, took the opportunity to check out the changing landscape. After a while, the desert ground began to soften and he spotted a few shrubs, then a few more. Soon the ground became lush and green and the shrubs gave way to taller trees. And then, up ahead, Simba saw a wall of green. He shook his head, not sure it wasn't just a mirage or a trick of his overheated brain and hungry stomach. But when his vision cleared, the wall of green was still there.

A moment later, Pumbaa pushed right through the trees and into the lush jungle beyond. As Simba followed, his eyes grew wide. He had never seen so many colors before in his life. Bright greens. Vibrant oranges. Pops of purple and ribbons of red. The Pride Lands were beautiful but they were sparse, the colors always muted, even in the wettest of seasons when the green grasses were at their brightest. But this place? This place looked like it was never dull. It was a paradise.

"Welcome to our humble home," Timon said, gesturing around him.

"You live here?" Simba said, shocked and awed.

Timon nodded. "We live wherever we want," he corrected.

"Do as we please," Pumbaa added.

Simba smiled. The jungle was beautiful. Maybe there was something to the *hakuna matata* mentality after all. If they got to live here . . .

Simba was still smiling as Pumbaa led him into a clearing. A giant tree dominated one side, its thick roots rising out of the ground, its long branches and heavy leaves providing a natural shelter. As Simba glanced around, he spotted a few animals loitering near the tree.

"Everyone," Timon shouted. "This is Simba!"

Immediately, the animals ducked out of sight. "Guys," Pumbaa called, "come out and say hello!" One by one, the small animals began to emerge from their hiding spots. They all looked terrified.

"We're all going to die!" an elephant shrew shouted in a squeaky voice. His long thin nose twitched wildly, and his eyes were so wide they were disproportionate to the rest of his small rodent body.

A honey badger, popping out from a hole in the ground, pointed at Simba. "That's a lion," he said, sneering and revealing his sharp teeth. But his voice shook and Simba could see that the white strip of fur on his otherwise black body was trembling.

"True," Pumbaa said, shrugging. "But it's a *little* lion."

Just then, a small dung beetle strolled by, pushing a dark round ball in front of him. The animals all crinkled their noses at the unpleasant scent of the dung beetle's "prize."

"Get out of here with that thing!" the honey badger snarled, forgetting to be concerned about Simba.

"I told you guys—it's just mud!" the dung beetle cried. "Well, mostly."

The other animals shook their heads. Simba tried not to smile as he heard them mumbling to themselves about the dung beetle and the ball in front of him. Noticing the lion was smiling, the other animals backed up nervously. The smile, while innocent, revealed a few too many of Simba's teeth.

"What about food?" a bush baby asked. Seeing Simba's teeth had made everyone think the same thing. "Have you thought about feeding that thing?"

At the mention of food, Simba's stomach let out a loud growl. "I'm starved," he said. "I could eat a whole zebra."

The clearing went silent. Even the dung beetle stopped rolling his ball. The animals froze. Simba watched, confused. Finally, Timon cleared his throat. "Uh, we're fresh out of zebra," he said, gesturing around the zebra-less clearing.

Simba's stomach let out another growl. He wasn't going to be picky. He just wanted something to eat, even if it wasn't his favorite. "Any antelope?" he asked hopefully.

Apparently, that was not the right request. Timon and Pumbaa both began to shake their heads while the smaller animals circled together defensively. "Listen, kid," Timon said. "If you want to live with us, you got to eat like us."

"And most importantly," the elephant shrew added in a small squeak, "not eat us!"

Gesturing for Simba to follow, Timon led him over to a fallen log. The wood was rotten in places and covered in moss in others. It had clearly been lying there on the clearing floor for a long time. "This looks like a good spot to rustle up some grub," Timon said confidently.

Simba looked down at the tree and then up at Pumbaa, who was standing next to him. He cocked his head. *This* looked like a good place to get food? It didn't look large enough to be hiding a zebra or an antelope—or even a small topi.

Catching Simba's look of bewilderment, Pumbaa lowered his head and hooked his tusks under the log. Then, with a grunt, he lifted it up. Simba took a startled step backward as he caught sight of thousands of insects squirming in the damp, dark ground. Some were pale, their bodies plump and slimy. Others were segmented, with hard shells and lots of feet. A few appeared to have wings, and Simba was pretty sure he saw a couple that had pincers. "Ew," he said, crinkling his nose in disgust. "What's that?" he asked, pointing to one of the rounder, plumper bugs.

"A grub," the honey badger answered. "What's it look like?"

"Gross," Simba answered. *Really,* really *gross,* he added silently.

To his surprise, Timon reached into the pile of bugs and picked up one of the round ones. Then, as Simba watched in horror, he popped it into his mouth. Simba swallowed back a wave of nausea.

"Mmm!" Timon said as he chewed. "Tastes like chicken."

Pumbaa grabbed his own food—a long worm that wriggled and squirmed—and slurped it up. "Slimy, yet satisfying."

One by one, the other animals joined in the feast. As Timon and Pumbaa continued to munch on their grubs of choice, the bush baby picked up one of the hard-shelled bugs and the honey badger scooped up a whole collection. They munched and crunched happily, unaware that the whole time, Simba was trying hard not to throw up. And to think he used to be picky about antelope. Compared to this, that seemed like the tastiest thing in the world!

Maybe this whole hakuna matata *thing isn't for me,* Simba thought. He couldn't imagine ever eating a single bug, let alone living off them. And while he liked Timon and Pumbaa, the other animals didn't seem so warm and fuzzy. An image of the den on Pride Rock and of snuggling with his family flashed unexpectedly through his mind. He couldn't imagine cuddling like that here, despite how beautiful the jungle was. Sadness began to creep back over him and he lowered his head, hoping no one would notice.

At that moment, Timon walked over, holding a huge leaf out in front of him. On it was a selection of bugs. "I'm telling ya, kid," he said, as though he knew Simba was having doubts, "this is the great life. No rules, no responsibilities. And the best of all, no worries." He lifted one of the plumpest bugs off the leaf and held it out to Simba. "Well, kid?"

Simba looked down at the bug, his mind racing. True, this was *not* Pride Rock. The bug was no antelope, and Timon and Pumbaa weren't Nala or his mother. But no worries? No responsibilities? Getting to forget all the bad things he had just run from? That *did* sound good. So maybe his life was going to be different. But at least he had a place to call home now. And maybe, hopefully, even some friends.

Taking a deep breath, he nodded. "Oh, well," he said, grabbing the bug. *"Hakuna matata!"* Opening his mouth and closing his eyes, he tossed the bug in. Then he began to chew. To his surprise, it wasn't so bad. He began to smile. "Slimy," he finally said, opening his eyes. "Yet satisfying."

As Timon and Pumbaa let out cheers, Simba grabbed another bug from the pile. *Yes,* he thought as he continued to eat, *this may not be what I imagined. But it is a heck of a lot better than being on my own.* Plopping down on the warm ground in front of the log, he listened as the other animals chatted and laughed while Pumbaa passed gas and Timon told them about the vulture bowling and saving Simba. Their voices faded in and out as the sun shone down through the canopy of trees, dappling the ground with light. It was peaceful. Simba's stomach was getting full and he was no longer as tired. In fact, for the first time since he had run from the Pride Lands, Simba felt something welling up in his chest that wasn't grief or heartache. He felt hope.

CHAPTER FOURTEEN

Time passed as Simba learned to adjust to his new life in the jungle. Timon, always happy to be the expert, took on the role of teacher. At least one part of every day was spent wandering through the jungle as Timon pointed out the various bugs and plants that could be found around the clearing. Some were okay to eat, others not (something Simba found out the hard way).

The clearing, Simba soon found out, was

near the edge of the deep jungle. The jungle itself went on for miles and miles and was full of amazing things. There was a huge waterfall that led to a deep pool, perfect for getting a drink or, if the occasion called for it—though it rarely did for his new friends—taking a bath. There were rivers that crisscrossed under the trees, and there was always ample shade. Used to sleeping tucked in the back of a dark den, it took some time for Simba to learn to sleep under the stars. But soon enough, he found the light comforting, the sounds of the jungle like a lullaby.

Pumbaa was in charge of Simba's "training." The warthog was a surprisingly stealthy hunter, despite his unfortunate habit of passing gas—loudly. As soon as Simba grew comfortable enough eating grubs, Pumbaa had him off learning to bowl for buzzards and snag the rare and delicious vulture egg.

"Stay low," Pumbaa said as they hid behind a pile of rocks, staring at a particularly ugly group of vultures. They had spotted the birds circling from the edge of the jungle earlier that day. When enough time had passed, according to Pumbaa, for the birds to eat and grow lazy, they trotted out into the desert.

"I know how to hunt," Simba whined. "Just let me do my thing. I'll show you how to *really* hunt." Before Pumbaa could stop him, he charged. Immediately, the birds took back to the air, and by the time he reached where they had been, they were once again circling.

Pumbaa trotted over, shaking his head. "You can't just run at them," he said, laughing. "They may be ugly, but they aren't stupid. And they have wings." Finding another pile of rocks downwind, he gestured for Simba to join him.

Once again, they lowered themselves to the ground. Only this time, Simba stayed down. As the sun rose higher and higher in the sky, he saw the birds begin to tuck their heads under their wings, drowsy from their feast and the sun. Gesturing for Simba to watch, Pumbaa began to tiptoe out from behind the rocks and over to the birds. His steps were light, and for such a heavy creature, he barely made any noise. When he was only a few feet away, he stopped, tilted back his head, and let out a shout. At the same time, he loudly passed gas.

The combination of booming noises startled the birds out of their sleep and Simba watched as once more they flew straight up into the air. Only this time, instead of circling, they flew away. When the sound of their flapping wings faded, Simba looked over to where Pumbaa stood. There, in front of him, were two huge eggs.

"Told ya," Pumbaa said. "You've just got to be patient." Then, leaning down, he picked the eggs up in his tusks and trotted back over. "Wait till Timon and the others see this!" he said happily. "Two eggs! We hit the jackpot. Now let's go home."

As they headed back to the clearing to share the meal, Simba shook his head. *Home.* The word no longer meant Pride Rock. It meant the clearing. And his family was now Timon and Pumbaa and the others. As the desert gave way to the green of the jungle, Simba realized that for the first time in weeks, the thought didn't bother him.

CHAPTER FOURTEEN

Thus, the days and years passed. Simba's legs grew longer. His mane grew thicker and his chest filled out. Even on a diet of grubs and berries, the cub was becoming a full-grown lion. Soon he didn't need to use the fallen log over the creek to get to the other side. Instead, he could simply leap over it. And while at first he had been comfortable and small enough to sleep snuggled between Timon and Pumbaa, he found that soon they were more comfortable sleeping on top of his large body.

Even the other animals, including the honey badger, the bush baby, and the elephant shrew, grew used to his presence—and his size. When they needed something on a branch that was too high to reach, it was Simba who could rise up on his back legs and get what they needed. If the occasional intruder found its way into the clearing, Simba's growl was enough to send it running.

It was peaceful in the clearing, and as time moved on, Simba spent less and less time thinking about his old life. Eventually, the memories became cloudy and faded. He was happy now. The past was in the past. Like Timon had taught him years before, there was no point in thinking about what had happened. *Hakuna matata.* It wasn't just a passing phrase for Simba and his new family. It was a way of life.

And he liked his new life a lot. He had all the food he could eat, a cozy place to sleep, friends to rely on, and no enemies to fight.

But sometimes, as he lay down to sleep and the stars shone down, he couldn't help wondering how the Pride Lands were—if Nala and his mother were looking up at the same stars, their own bellies full, safe in the mouth of Pride Rock, and wondering what had happened to him.

Nala looked out over the Pride Lands—or rather, what was left of them—and crinkled her nose in disgust. In the distance, she could make out a group of mangy hyenas chasing off a herd of topis. Even from the top of Pride Rock, she could hear their terrible cackles and the frightened cries of the topis.

She shook her head. How had it come to this?

The answer was simple: Scar.

In the years since he had taken over the pride, he had destroyed everything Mufasa had worked so hard to create. The savannah grasses, what was left of them, were short and brown, trampled down by the hyenas' constant chases and the terrified herds who had run—and kept on running. The Pride Lands were nearly empty, looking more like the Elephant Graveyard now than the fertile region they had once been. Dried bones littered the landscape and the few animals who had stayed were thin and weak as a result of their food being taken and eaten by the hyenas. The watering hole, which Scar did nothing to monitor, had been drained nearly dry. All that remained was a puddle, the hippos that had needed it to survive long since gone.

Sighing, Nala looked over her shoulder at the other

lionesses. They, too, were mere shadows of the proud and beautiful creatures they had once been. Lack of food and water, coupled with exhaustion from being sent to hunt far too often, had left them weak. Their fur was dull, their eyes lifeless.

As Nala looked at her family and friends, she felt a familiar surge of rage bubble up inside her. She hated Scar. She hated what he had done to her and to Sarabi and to all the animals of the Pride Lands. He was a terrible, selfish creature, and not for the first time, she thought of what life would have been like if Simba had survived. *If he were here,* she thought, *none of this would have happened.*

Thinking of her old friend, Nala's eyes welled with tears. Losing him had been the hardest thing she had ever gone through. It still hurt more than the constant ache in her stomach or the pads of her paws worn bloody from long, useless hunts on the hard ground.

At first, back when she and the others had heard the news of Simba's and Mufasa's deaths, Nala had clung to the hope that somehow, someway, Simba would return. She had believed Sarabi when the queen had said they would be okay, and she had even tried to give Scar a chance. But the hope had faded fast. She missed her friend. She hated going to the watering hole without him; she dreaded bath times without him there to make her laugh. Even teasing Zazu quickly lost its appeal. Without Simba, Nala felt like her life had become duller.

As Scar continued to let the hyenas take over more and more of the Pride Lands, and as it became clearer and clearer that there was nothing the lionesses could do to stop them, Nala stopped pining for her friend. Instead, she became fixated on finding someone, anyone, who could help. That thought alone, of bringing a lion back to the Pride Lands to destroy Scar, fueled Nala's dreams and kept her focused during the days that slipped into years, while all around her life grew harder and even Sarabi gave up trying.

Each night, Nala would stare up at the star-filled sky. Simba had told her what his father had said all those years before—that the great kings looked down on them. She had to believe that they did, and that somehow they were still looking out for the Pride Lands, despite Scar and his hyenas.

But it was growing harder to believe. And now, as she watched yet another herd leave the Pride Lands for somewhere safer, a bit more of her hope disappeared. If someone didn't do something soon, there would be no Pride Lands left to save.

Hearing the sound of flapping wings, Nala looked up and a bit of light returned to her eyes. While much had changed, there was one thing that had remained the same—Zazu. The hornbill refused to report to Scar and remained loyal to Sarabi. Every morning, without fail, he reported in—whether the news was good or bad, though it was mostly bad.

Smiling as Zazu landed beside her, Nala waited for Sarabi to approach. The queen still carried her head high, and even though her ribs were visible beneath her fading fur, she walked gracefully. "The morning report, Zazu," she said, nodding her head in greeting.

"Your Majesty," Zazu said with a nod of his own.

"The Pride Lands are in imminent danger. The hyenas are chasing off the last of the herds."

Just as he finished, Azizi and Kamari charged up onto Pride Rock. Letting out a series of snarls and yips, they went right after Zazu. The hornbill took to the air, staying safely out of harm's way. A moment later, Scar appeared.

"Good morning, ladies," he drawled as he walked past the lionesses and headed toward the edge of Pride Rock. While the lionesses were nearly skin and bones, Scar had grown bigger in the years since he had taken over the Pride Lands—though he still looked small and weak compared to the lion Mufasa had been.

Nala watched him flop down on the warm stone, and her eyes narrowed. A fresh wave of hate washed over her as Scar began to groom himself leisurely, as though he had not a care in the world, while down below the lands he was supposed to protect grew worse. "We *have* to do something, Sarabi," Nala said, her jaw clenched tight. "We have to fight!"

Sarabi shook her head. "Nala," she said, her voice

measured. The two lionesses had had this conversation many times before. "Scar is our king."

"But *you* are the queen!" Nala said. "We should leave, before it's too late."

"We must all stay together and protect the Pride Lands," Sarabi said, keeping her voice low so as not to attract Scar's attention. "This is our home, Nala. We can never abandon it."

Nala bit back the scream that threatened to pour from her throat. How could Sarabi say that? This wasn't their home—at least not anymore. This was a terrible shadow of the place they had once called home.

"Sarabi."

Shenzi's voice broke through Nala's thoughts, and she looked up to see the queen of the hyenas standing a few feet away. Her cold eyes were narrowed as she looked at the two lionesses. "The king wishes to see you."

Looking over to where Scar stood, his grooming session over, Nala shook her head. "Don't go," she said to Sarabi.

CHAPTER FOURTEEN

"I'm not afraid of him," Sarabi answered as she lifted her head and began to follow Shenzi.

Nala watched her go. *I'm not afraid of him, either.* The words she wished she had said flashed through her mind. *But he isn't our king. And we should never come when he calls. He doesn't deserve that respect. He doesn't deserve any of this. . . .*

Sarabi's nose crinkled as she approached Scar. The smell of blood was thick in the air. His back to her, his head lowered, Scar helped himself to a bite of the fresh kill the lionesses had managed to take down in the deep of the night.

Hearing her footsteps, Scar looked up. "Won't you join me, Sarabi?" he said, nodding to the kill. "There is plenty to go around."

Sarabi shook her head, her eyes traveling past Scar to the Pride Lands beyond. Vultures circled in the dark sky, and the ground was littered with decay. "You're overhunting, Scar," she said, trying to keep her voice level. She knew Nala thought she was weak for talking to him, that she didn't care as much as the young lioness did. But she did care. Seeing what Scar had done to this place was almost as terrible as losing Mufasa and Simba. It broke her heart anew every morning when she awoke to find the devastation Scar had wrought. But she had learned from Mufasa that some battles were meant to be waged over time, and this was one such battle. It would do her no good to outwardly hate Scar. But that didn't mean she couldn't hate him on the inside—with every fiber of her being.

Scar brushed off Sarabi's observation. "I've simply perfected the kill," he said, "with the help of my army."

"You're destroying it all!" The words were out of her mouth before Sarabi could stop herself.

But Scar didn't grow angry at the impertinence. Instead, he laughed. "Don't you see?" he said, still chuckling. "There is nobody to challenge me. We can finally take whatever we want."

Sarabi raised an eyebrow. "We?" she repeated.

Scar nodded. "Long ago, you chose Mufasa over

me," he said, his laughter fading and a dark look entering his eye. "But now there is a new king—so stop being so selfish."

"You are the selfish one," Sarabi snapped, this time not bothering to hide her disgust.

"The other lions look to you," Scar said. His voice was still calm, but Sarabi could see it strained the lion to keep his cool. "As long as you resist, they will reject me. Take your place by my side—and we will feast together!" He stopped and looked over at her.

Over the years, Scar had said this same thing many times. In the beginning, her refusals had been quick, furious, and absolute. She was Mufasa's queen and would never be anyone else's. But as she looked at the food Scar so casually ate, her stomach growling, she realized it was growing harder and harder to say no. She knew that his promises were false. There was no way, even if she agreed to become his queen, that he would share his food and resources with the other lionesses. His army of hyenas would never allow it. Still, a part of her wondered if maybe the only way to give the other lionesses hope would be to take him up on his offer.

But as suddenly as the horrible thought entered her consciousness, it disappeared. She shook her head. There was no way she would ever agree. "I told you," she said. "I will never be your queen!"

Abandoning the kill, Scar rose to his full height. He looked down at Sarabi and slowly shook his head. Her response didn't seem to surprise him, but his answer caught her off guard. "Then from now on," he said, walking past her, "the lions will eat after the hyenas." Gesturing to Shenzi and the others, he watched as they raced by him and dove into the kill. The sound of their snarls filled the air as they began to devour the food. He watched for a moment and then turned back to Sarabi. "And they don't leave much behind."

Without another word, Scar slunk into the den. Sarabi watched him go, a terrible feeling welling up inside her. What had she just done?

CHAPTER FIFTEEN

The jungle was quiet. Above, the sun shone down through clouds. Its strong rays were muted, making the temperature comfortable. On the ground, animals took advantage of the day and meandered out of their nests or dens to eat.

Walking into a circle of trees, an impala lifted his head and nibbled at some leaves. His long horns rustled the branches, and as the clouds moved, the sun shone down on the animal's golden brown coat.

Suddenly, the peace was broken as somewhere nearby, a twig snapped.

Instantly, the impala froze. His brown eyes grew wide as he scanned the trees beyond and the longer grasses close by. Seeing nothing, the impala was just about to go back to eating when a huge lion leapt out of the grasses right at him.

The impala screamed and jumped into a large bush.

The lion stopped in his tracks. Then he smiled. “Hey,” Simba said to the impala. “You see that? I almost caught that butterfly!” Then he cocked his head. “Why are you in the bushes?” He was unaware that, to the impala, he looked like a real predator—not the friendly lion everyone had grown to love in the jungle.

As the impala said a shaky good-bye and sprinted off, Simba watched, confused. He was still staring at where the impala had disappeared into the trees when Timon and Pumbaa ambled over. Seeing that his friend looked upset, Timon put a hand on Simba’s mane, now long, thick, and deep red.

"Simba," he said, shaking his head, "a guy like that will never frolic with a guy like you."

"Why not?" Simba asked, genuinely perplexed. He didn't understand. He had wanted to catch the butterfly, not hurt the impala.

Gesturing for him to follow, Timon began to walk back toward their clearing. For a while, the trio was silent, and Simba's thoughts drifted like the clouds above. It had been years since any of his friends had made him feel like the outcast he had been when he'd come to the jungle. In the beginning, he had known that the honey badger and the elephant shrew, and even the dung beetle, were wary of him. They saw him as a vicious lion, even if he was a cub. But over the years, even they had become used to him. He no longer made them nervous: he didn't send the elephant shrew ducking into a hole when he pounced at a shadow; he didn't make the white fur on the honey badger's back rise; he didn't scare the bush baby when a yawn accidentally turned into a roar. But moments like this reminded him he was still a lion, even if he didn't belong to a pride.

As they passed by a large termite mound, he saw his other friends hunched around it, each desperately trying to get inside. Timon followed Simba's gaze and nodded. "You see," he said, continuing the conversation he had started earlier, "in nature there's a delicate balance."

Simba narrowed his eyes. "I know all about the Circle of Life." He hadn't thought about it or said those words aloud in years, but he remembered it all too well. It was what had taken his father away from him. His father. He hadn't thought about him in a long, long time. Shaking off the feeling of sadness that he felt beginning to form, he ran over to the termite mound and slammed his body into the side. It broke open, termites pouring out.

Timon cocked his head. "Circle?" he said as he shoveled termites into his mouth. "What circle? I'm talking about the Meaningless Line of Indifference."

CHAPTER FIFTEEN

"You see, there's this straight line," Pumbaa explained. "And we all run toward it in paralyzing fear."

Simba tried not to laugh as his friend demonstrated. Widening his eyes, the warthog opened his mouth and put his hoofs to his cheeks. Then he took off running—right into a tree. He slammed into it and bounced backward, landing with a thud.

"And it leads to nothing," Timon continued as Pumbaa shook his head and trotted back over.

"Because it's a meaningless line," Pumbaa added.

"Of indifference," Timon finished.

Simba walked over and began tearing some bark off a tree. As bugs rained down, he grabbed a handful and turned back to his friends. "You *sure* it's not a circle?" he asked. Was it possible he had forgotten the lesson his father had taught him? He shook his head. No, it had been a circle. "We're all connected . . ." he pressed.

This time it was Pumbaa's turn to look confused.

"You're not making any sense!" he said. "A circle would mean that what I did mattered to everyone else"—he let out a laugh, and then a fart—"which is ridiculous."

Before Simba could point out that Pumbaa did, in fact, matter to him, Timon went on. "Now go ahead, Simba," he said, clapping his hands together and hopping up and down excitedly. "For the first time we're entrusting you to make a plan for us today."

"This is important," Pumbaa added. "Think about all you've been taught. The straight line leads to . . ."

"Absolutely nothing?" Simba answered, finishing Pumbaa's sentence.

Apparently, that was exactly the right thing to say, because everyone cheered. It looked like they had another long day of doing nothing to look forward to. As Simba shoved another handful of termites in his mouth, he smiled. Maybe Timon and Pumbaa were onto something. A straight line of not caring was a heck of a lot better than a circle of caring too much.

CHAPTER FIFTEEN

The sun had long since set on their leisurely day as Simba, Timon, and Pumbaa lay on their backs in the middle of the clearing. Stars twinkled brilliantly in the sky above and a gentle breeze blew through the jungle, making the leaves whisper. It was quiet and beautiful.

And then, Simba burped.

"Whoa!" Timon cried. "Nice one!"

Simba smiled proudly. "Thanks," he said, sounding pleased by the praise. "Must have been the termites."

In answer, Pumbaa let out a loud, long fart. "Or the crickets," he said, laughing.

"And you wonder why I prefer to sleep underground," Timon said, waving a hand in front of his nose. But he smiled as he said it, not really bothered by his friends' interruption. He was more than used to it at this point.

Silence once more fell over the group, and for a long moment, the only noise was the sound of the friends' breathing. Then Pumbaa turned his head and looked over at Timon. "You ever look up and wonder what those sparkly dots are up there?" he asked, his voice soft.

"Pumbaa," Timon replied, "I don't wonder. I know."

"Oh," Pumbaa breathed, impressed. "What are they?"

Timon sat up and cleared his throat, eager as always to show the others how much he knew. "They're fireflies," he explained. "Fireflies that got stuck on that big bluish-black thing."

Pumbaa frowned slightly. That wasn't the answer he had been expecting. He thought the sparkly dots were something much different. "I always thought they were balls of gas, burning billions of miles away."

Simba half-listened to his friends as they playfully bickered, each confident that they knew the right answer. But his gaze remained trained on the sky above, a hazy memory of a night long ago tickling at his mind. A memory of staring up at this same sky on a peaceful night just like this one. A memory of something good before things went terribly wrong.

"What do you think, Simba?"

Timon's question startled Simba out of his reverie. "Well, I don't know," he said softly. "Somebody once told me the great kings of the past are up there—watching over us."

There was a long pause, and then Timon and Pumbaa burst out laughing. "That's a good one," Pumbaa said, clutching his sides and rolling around.

"Royal dead guys watching over us!" Timon cracked, his eyes watering from laughing so hard. "I hope they don't fall out of the sky!" He held his hands over his head and pretended to duck out of the way. Finally regaining his composure, he looked over at Simba. "Think about it. Why would a bunch of kings be looking out for us? We're outcasts."

Getting to his feet, Simba shook his head. He knew his friends didn't mean anything by it, but hearing them laugh at his father's words hurt more than he would have expected it to. It hit a nerve that he'd thought had long since gone numb. Turning his back on Timon and Pumbaa, he slowly began to walk away. He needed some time alone.

The air was still as he walked out of the clearing and over to a nearby hill. The spot had become his favorite place over the years. Out of the way, and with few hiding spots, it was usually empty and afforded Simba a view out over the horizon. When he was younger, the hill had been as close to Pride Rock as he could find. He had spent hours lying up on the edge, looking out, wondering, hoping that maybe, somehow, his father would appear on the ground below. He would imagine Nala bursting through the brush, her big green eyes full of warm laughter. During the worst moments, he would find himself thinking of his mother, missing her warmth.

Reaching the top of the hill, he ambled over to the edge and flopped down. The movement sent a puff of dust up into the air and Simba watched as it floated farther and farther away until it disappeared altogether. Only then did he dare lift his head.

The stars shone down, appearing closer now from his new vantage point. A sad, soft sigh slipped from his mouth as, in the gentle breeze, he once again heard his father's voice and felt his mother's touch. To his surprise, he felt his eyes well up, a single tear falling down his face. He hadn't cried in so long and the reaction made him upset. Angrily, he swiped away the tear, sending a tuft of his own fur flying into the air.

He knew he wasn't angry. If he was honest with himself, he was just sad. Sad that even now, years later, he couldn't escape the ghosts of his past. Somehow, Mufasa was always there, right at the periphery, his deep voice the conscience in Simba's head. He was the voice that tried to make Simba do something when Timon and Pumbaa were content to do nothing. Simba's memories of Pride Rock and the life he had lived there kept a piece of him from ever truly embracing the *hakuna matata* way of thinking.

Shaking his head, he tried to stop the flood of emotions he felt cascading to the surface. He didn't want to worry or think about Pride Rock. He doubted anyone was thinking about him there. The lionesses were probably busy hunting, the herds busy feeding. He imagined Zazu was still making his reports about the day-to-day successes of the Pride Lands. And Nala? Well, she was probably running around with a new best friend, chasing hippos and ducking in and out of the brush beside the overflowing watering hole.

Simba stood up. No, it wasn't worth thinking about the past. The past was in the past. The stars were probably fireflies caught on a big black nothing. And he would be better off going back to the clearing—his home.

CHAPTER SIXTEEN

Nala opened her eyes. Around her, she could hear the even breathing of the other lionesses, and beyond that, the snores of the surrounding hyenas. Getting to her feet, she softly padded around the sleeping bodies of her friends and made her way to the front of the den.

Sarabi was awake, her head up, silently looking out over the desolated Pride Lands. Her eyes were dark and full of emotion. Even in the middle of the night, it was clear how much damage Scar and the hyenas had caused. There were no sounds of nocturnal animals calling to each other, no occasional birdcalls or trumpeting elephants. Those animals were all long gone. The only life left in the Pride Lands were the lions, the hyenas, and the few remaining lone souls who still dared try to make a home there.

Slowly, Sarabi turned her head and looked over at the younger lioness. "Are you sure I can't change your mind?" she whispered.

Nala shook her head. She knew Sarabi had been dreading this moment for a long time. But they had no choice. Things had grown too dire. Something needed to change, and while it wasn't Nala's first choice to be the one to go, no one else had offered. In stolen moments, they had whispered plans, discussed possibilities that did not involve Nala leaving. But time and time again, they had come to the same conclusion—or rather, Nala had come to her own conclusion.

"I have to look for help, Sarabi," she said now. "I

have to try. Tell my mother not to worry—I promise to come back."

Nala turned to go but hesitated. Looking over the tired lionesses, their ribs visible, their bodies relaxed only now in sleep, her eyes welled with unspoken emotion. They had been through so much. They had suffered unnecessarily and seen the land they loved ruined. She couldn't let them down.

But as she tiptoed past the sleeping lions and toward the small hole in the back of the cave, she couldn't help wondering—what if there was no one out there who would help them? What if she failed? What would happen to the Pride Lands? And most importantly, what would happen to Sarabi and her mother and all the other lionesses? She paused at the opening and took one last look behind her.

Shaking her head, Nala ducked out of the cave. Then, taking a deep breath, she slipped into the darkness of the night, leaving the sleeping hyenas and her pride of loyal lionesses behind.

I will *be back,* she vowed to herself as the snores of the hyenas faded and the night grew silent. *I promise. I'll get help, no matter how long it takes me or how far I have to go. The answer* has *to be out there. Somewhere.*

A night of sleep had done wonders for Simba's attitude, and he woke up ready to put his past in the past—again. Jumping to his feet, he had yawned, stretched, and shaken his mane out of his eyes. Then he had grabbed a few grubs and sat down to think. He felt like doing something today. Not something *too* big. But maybe a walk through the jungle? It'd do his friends some good to get out of the clearing.

With this plan in mind, he woke up Timon and Pumbaa and soon the trio were making their way through the jungle. It was quiet in the early morning, the jungle animals still tucked safely in their holes, dens, and caves. Simba strolled along, content to enjoy the peace and quiet.

And then Timon began to sing.

Tilting back his head, he started to warble. As he got into it, his voice grew louder and more off-key. Simba started to laugh. By the time the meerkat hit the chorus, Pumbaa had joined in and Simba was swinging his head to the bouncy rhythm.

As the trio continued their impromptu concert, Pumbaa closed his eyes and sang the loudest. Caught up in the song, Simba didn't even realize the warthog had wandered away—until he heard him scream. Loudly.

Instantly, Simba stopped singing. His head spun around as he looked to see what had caused his friend to let out such a frightened scream. To his surprise and horror, the reason was immediately apparent. A lioness, her hackles raised and her teeth bared, was chasing Pumbaa across the jungle floor.

In a blind panic, Pumbaa sprinted as fast as his little legs could take him, running around a series of fallen logs and over a jumble of rocks. But he wasn't fast enough. In moments, the lioness had him cornered against a tree.

Not stopping to think, Simba charged after his friend. Leaping over the same logs, he spotted a low-hanging branch a few feet above where Pumbaa was cowering. He jumped up on it, raced across, and then, just as the lioness was about to pounce, flung himself off the tree.

The air rushed from his lungs as he landed with a thud right on top of the lioness. The momentum sent them both flying across the leafy ground. They rolled head over tail for a few feet, snarling and wrestling, each trying to get the upper hand until, finally, the lioness flipped Simba over onto his back. Pinned to the ground, Simba struggled to get free. But the lioness was stronger than she appeared, and the harder he struggled, the fiercer she looked.

And then, to his surprise, the lioness's grip loosened. Her eyes grew wide and her breath hitched. "Simba?" she said, jumping off him and backing away.

As his name left her mouth, Simba's own eyes grew wide. Could it be? Was it even possible? He shook his head, trying to see if his vision was impaired. But when he stopped, he was still looking at the same green eyes that were now obviously and clearly familiar. "Nala?" he said in disbelief.

"Is that really you?" she asked, echoing the thought in his own head.

Getting to his feet, Simba nodded. "It's me!" he cried, racing forward and throwing his paws around Nala. He felt hysterical laughter bubble up inside him. Nala was there! In the jungle!

"Simba!" she said, pulling back. Her eyes grew suddenly serious, causing Simba's laughter to catch in his throat. "I thought you were dead!"

Dead? What did she mean she thought he was dead? What had Scar told her? His mind raced. When he had first arrived in the jungle, he had dreamed of this moment. But in time the dream had faded, and he had come to grips with the fact that Nala and the others had moved on, never thought of him. But could he have been wrong? He looked up at Nala, not sure what to say.

"I thought *I* was dead," Pumbaa said, interrupting the moment. He was still standing by the tree, shaking.

"What is going on here?" Timon piped up, looking back and forth between the two lions, bewilderment making his big eyes bigger.

Shaking off his confusion, Simba turned to his friends. "Timon, Pumbaa," he said, "I want you to meet my best friend—Nala."

Timon raised a hand to his heart. "Best friend?" he repeated. "That hurts."

"Nala is such a pretty name," Pumbaa said, immediately okay with the lioness now that she wasn't trying to kill him.

But Timon was not as easy to appease. He kept looking back and forth between Nala and Simba, shaking his head. "Let me get this straight," he finally said. "You know her. She knows you. But she wants to eat him." He pointed at Pumbaa, who shrugged. "And everyone is okay with this? Did I miss something?"

"It's a pleasure to meet you, Nala," Pumbaa went on, ignoring his friend.

"Don't say meat!" Timon shouted. "She's looking at you like a full rack of ribs."

CHAPTER SIXTEEN

Simba had to admit Timon wasn't wrong. Nala *was* looking at Pumbaa like he might make a good snack. But Simba knew she wouldn't hurt him. She was Nala. His buddy. His best friend. Even if she did look a little hungrier and skinnier than he would have imagined, she wouldn't hurt anyone Simba cared about. He would show her the nearest fallen log and get her a good snack. "This is incredible!" he finally said, no longer able to contain his excitement. "You're going to love it here!"

Nala cocked her head, looking confused. "Simba," she said, shaking her head. "We need to leave. Scar has taken over with the hyenas. You *have* to take your place as king!"

Simba stared at Nala. Now that his excitement was fading, he realized she looked scared. And tired. But was she really suggesting he go back and become king? He couldn't go back. He didn't belong there. That was his old life. He started to shake his head, but before he could speak, Timon jumped in.

"King? Simba?" he said. "Lady, have you got your lions crossed?"

Pumbaa, on the other hand, didn't seem to think it was such a crazy idea. Bending over, he lowered his head and bowed.

"Pumbaa," Simba said, walking over and lifting the warthog's head. "She's wrong."

Simba felt Nala's gaze on him, but he didn't turn around. Instead, he began to pace. How could this moment have gone from amazing to terrible so quickly? Seeing Nala was amazing. But being reminded of what he had left? That was terrible.

"Seeing you again," Nala pressed. "You don't know what this will mean to everyone. You have to come home."

Simba shook his head. "This is my home," he said. Moving toward her, he stopped right in front of her. Their eyes locked, and for a moment, Simba forgot what he was going to say. In the dappled light, Nala looked . . . different. She still looked like the best friend he had left behind, but at the same time she seemed wiser, tougher, stronger. She looked like she had carried a heavy weight on her shoulders for a long time. But she didn't need to, not if she stayed in the jungle. "Please stay," he finally said. "This place is incredible. I know you'll love it."

"I can't—" Nala started to say.

"Come on," Simba begged. "At least let me show you around!" He opened his eyes and pretended to pout, the same way he had when they were cubs and he'd wanted her to help him do something she knew she shouldn't. A small smile started to spread over her face, and finally, she gave the slightest of nods.

That was all Simba needed. Turning, he began to walk. He needed to show her how amazing the jungle was, how beautiful it could be. Because for some reason he couldn't quite explain, he really, *really* wanted her to stay—forever.

CHAPTER SEVENTEEN

Nala followed behind Simba, her mind racing. She had left the Pride Lands to find help. And she had ended up finding Simba. It was better than she could have imagined. In that moment, when she had first realized who he was, Nala had felt a surge of hope so big it threatened to drown her. But then he had been so quiet when she had told him what was happening at home, and he'd inexplicably refused to leave. She just didn't understand. What was so special about this place?

In the bushes behind them, she could hear Timon and Pumbaa talking about them. Or rather, she could hear the meerkat talking about *her*. She frowned as he told Pumbaa that nothing good would come of her showing up. Clearly, she was no threat. She had already asked Simba to come home and he had already said no.

Sighing, she shook off her sadness and picked up the pace. She might as well enjoy whatever time she had with Simba now, while she could. Looking ahead, she saw that he had stopped by the side of a river. The water rushed past, glimmering in the sunshine and creating small, nearly imperceptible rainbows near the surface. Nala's breath caught in her throat as a beam of light burst from between the clouds and illuminated Simba. In that moment, he looked nothing like the cub she had once known; he looked like his father. Powerful and strong, he looked every inch the king he should be—if only he would see it.

Unaware of Nala's thoughts, or the odd feeling

growing in her that she couldn't quite explain, Simba reached down and swiped a paw in the water, splashing her. Letting out a laugh, she ran over to him and swiped her own paw in the river. In moments, they were playing and giggling, just like they had down at the watering hole years ago.

For the rest of the afternoon, Nala followed Simba as he showed her the jungle he called home. After years of living under Scar's rule, watching the once fertile Pride Lands grow sparse and lifeless, the jungle provided her with welcome relief. The trees, thick with green leaves, covered soft ground that didn't hurt to walk on. The air was sweet with the smell of dozens of different plants and humid from the waterfalls that cascaded down from the high hills above. Taking off across an open field, Nala smiled, not only at Simba, who raced ahead, ducking and weaving between flowers with the abandon of a young cub, but also at the beauty all around her. She could see why Simba loved it there. She could even see how happy he seemed.

Ducking back into the trees, she jumped up onto a

branch and watched as Simba searched for her, their childhood game of hide-and-seek both familiar and different at the same time. From her vantage point, she saw his thick mane, broad shoulders, and powerful muscles that rippled beneath his golden fur. Feeling her gaze on him, he looked up and smiled warmly.

But even as the afternoon light faded to the glow of the early evening, Nala couldn't help thinking there was something Simba was keeping from her. She couldn't figure out what he was holding back, but every time they got too close, he would pull away. Every time she opened her mouth to even mention the Pride Lands, the smile would fade and his eyes would grow darker.

I just wish he would talk to me, Nala thought as they began to walk back along the small creek that led to the clearing. *If he told me what was going on, I could help—I think. . . .*

"Nala," Simba said, breaking the comfortable silence they had fallen into. "Isn't it great here? I want you to stay."

She nodded. “It’s amazing,” she agreed. “There’s just something I don’t understand.” She paused, not sure if she should go on and ruin the moment. But then she shook her head. She needed to know. “If you’ve been alive all this time, why haven’t you come home? We’ve really needed you.”

“Nobody needs me,” Simba said, his voice so full of sadness that Nala felt her own heart break.

“You’re the king,” she said softly. *Everybody needs you,* she added silently.

“Scar is the king,” Simba corrected.

Anger suddenly flooded through Nala. Anger at Simba for not seeing what was in front of him. Anger at Scar. Anger at everything. “Simba, he’s decimated the Pride Lands,” she said, no longer bothering to hold back. “There’s no food, no water—”

“There’s nothing I can do,” Simba said, interrupting her. He turned from the water and began to stalk into the jungle. His shoulders were tense, and she could tell he was struggling with some emotion he didn’t want her to see.

A part of Nala, a new part she was still trying to figure out, wanted to go to Simba and comfort him. But another part, a bigger part, was too angry. "What about your mother, Simba?" she said, hoping the mention of Sarabi would get through whatever walls Simba had put up around his heart. "This is your responsibility. You *need* to challenge Scar!"

"No," Simba said, shaking his head. "I can't go back. Ever."

"Why?" Nala pleaded. "Because of what happened in the gorge? Scar told us—"

"You wouldn't understand," Simba snapped. Then, shaking his head, he moved farther away. "None of it matters. *Hakuna matata.*"

Simba was right. She didn't understand. *Hakuna matata?* What was he talking about? Why was he so bent on not returning and becoming king? Her face must have shown her confusion because Simba went on.

"It's something I learned out here," he explained. "You see, sometimes bad things happen and there's nothing you can do about it. So why worry?"

"Why worry?" Nala repeated, shaking her head. She stared at Simba for a long moment, trying to see the cub she had known. But all she could see now was a stranger. A lion who was willing to turn his back on his family because he didn't want to "worry." An image of Simba, full of life, trailing after his father with adoration in his eyes flashed through Nala's mind. That Simba would never have said no to a fight. Never. "What happened to you?" she finally said out loud. "You're not the Simba I remember."

Simba shrugged. "And I never will be!" he said. "Are you satisfied?"

"No," Nala said sadly. "I'm disappointed."

"Well, now you're starting to sound like my father!" he said with a sudden fierceness in his voice that startled Nala.

She pressed on, not caring that she had struck a nerve. Simba had struck plenty in her. He deserved to hear what she said next. "Good—I'm glad one of us is."

To her surprise, the words seemed to get through to Simba. His head rose. The tension that had been building between them grew thicker. "You have no idea what I've been through!" he said, his voice raw, his eyes brimming.

Nala sighed. She didn't. Because he wouldn't tell her! But if he chose to keep his secrets, there was nothing more she could do. "And you have no idea how hard this is to say. I'm leaving . . . at sunrise." With one last look at Simba, she turned and began to walk away into the dense jungle beyond the shore of the creek. In moments, she was enveloped by the darkness. She paused, hoping that perhaps Simba would come after her. But after a few minutes, the jungle remained quiet.

With another sigh, Nala continued on. She had tried—and failed. And now she had to return to the Pride Lands and tell Sarabi she had found Simba, only to lose him all over again.

Night had come to the jungle. The animals were tucked in and the trees were quiet. Walking alone, his head hung low, Simba felt his throat close and his eyes well with tears. Why had Nala come back? What good had it done? All he could feel now was the sadness he had tried to keep at bay for so long.

He had heard everything she'd said, and while he had tried not to show it, hearing that the pride was suffering, that the Pride Lands were decimated, that his mother was in anguish, had slowly broken every bit of his heart there was left to break. But what good could he do? If he went back, it would only serve to make things worse. He had wanted to explain everything to Nala in the hopes that if she knew the truth, she might at least understand his decision. But every time he had started to say something, for some reason, he'd held back.

Angrily, he shook his head, hoping to dislodge the thoughts still swirling so violently inside. This was *not* the way Timon and Pumbaa had taught him to live. The past was in the past. He just needed to keep it there. But Nala had gone and dredged it all back up.

Suddenly, a strange noise came on the wind. It

startled Simba and he stopped, looking up, his head cocked. He had heard the sound before. It was almost like a chant, or a song. Curious, he made his way to the edge of the clearing and looked into the trees beyond.

At first, Simba saw nothing. But as his eyes adjusted, he made out the silhouette of a tall, lean monkey, his shoulders hunched with age, sitting on the branches of a nearby tree. And he was singing to himself.

Following the sound of the monkey's voice, Simba walked deeper into the jungle. But just as he got close to him, the monkey jumped to another tree. And then another. And another. Below, Simba chased after him, the sound of the monkey's crazed—and oddly familiar—laughter echoing through the jungle.

And then, just like that, the laughter stopped and the monkey disappeared. It was as though he had simply vanished into thin air. *Maybe I'm hallucinating,* Simba thought, shaking his head. *Maybe this is all a weird dream and I'm thinking about things from my old life because of Nala. . . .* But as he turned around, he saw that the monkey was back, sitting in another branch of a tree.

"Would you cut it out?" Simba shouted in frustration.

The monkey just laughed. "If you cut it out, it just grows back," he said mysteriously.

"Go away, creepy monkey!"

This time the monkey didn't laugh. Instead, he bopped himself upside the head with a large wooden cane he held in one of his hands. "Going away will not answer the question!"

"What question?" Simba said. He was getting a bit tired of this. "Who are you?"

"I know exactly who I am," the monkey said. "The question is—who are you?"

Simba shook his head. "I'm nobody!" he shouted. "So leave me alone!"

"Everybody is somebody," the monkey answered, not fazed by the angry lion. "Even a nobody."

"I think you're confused," Simba said. That could be the only explanation.

"I'm confused?" the monkey replied. Then he let

out another crazy laugh. "You don't even know who you are!"

"And I suppose you do!" Simba snapped, the last thread of his patience almost broken.

Jumping down from the tree, the old monkey walked forward, swinging his stick in front of him and humming. When he was right in front of Simba, he stopped—and smiled. "I held the son of Mufasa," he said.

The words struck Simba harder than if the monkey had hit him with the stick. "You knew my father?" he said softly.

"Correction," the monkey replied. "I *know* your father."

The jungle grew quiet as Simba stared at the monkey in front of him. How could he know Simba's father? That wasn't possible. His father had died a long time ago. Who did this crazy creature think he was, coming here and saying something so obviously untrue?

Rafiki.

The name came to Simba like a sudden punch. Rafiki. His father's friend and advisor. The mandrill who had introduced Simba to the Pride Lands and who had always fascinated him with his odd singing and strange way of talking. This monkey was Rafiki.

Seeing the recognition in Simba's eyes, Rafiki nodded slowly. "He's alive," the monkey said. "And I can take you to him. Follow me, I'll show!" He paused, a sly smile spreading across his wise face. "If you can keep up!"

Not waiting to see if Simba would follow, Rafiki took off. As he ran, his laughter bounced off the trees. Simba didn't hesitate. His heart pounding, he chased after Rafiki. He barely felt the branches of the bushes slapping at his face as he flew through the jungle. All he could hear was Rafiki's words bouncing through his head—his father was *alive*. Was it possible? Could it be? Doubt nagged at him, slowing his steps.

"Your father is waiting!" Rafiki shouted over his shoulder. "You better hurry!"

"Wait!" shouted Simba. But Rafiki kept going, swinging from tree to tree. For an old monkey, he was remarkably fast, and Simba struggled to keep up.

Finally, though, Rafiki came to a stop. Gasping for breath, Simba raised his head. Rafiki was standing in front of a small pond. He gestured to the still water. "Do you see him?"

Simba looked around, confused. He didn't see anything. Besides the pond, Rafiki, and a few low shrubs, they were completely alone. He shook his head. "I don't see anything."

"Look closer," Rafiki said, pointing his wooden staff at the pond.

Slowly, Simba walked over and looked down into the water. A breeze stirred the air and caused small ripples to move across the liquid surface. Simba's eyes narrowed. He still didn't see anything. But then, as the water settled, Simba saw his own reflection. Wavy at first, it grew clearer as the water stilled.

It had been years since Simba had looked down at his own reflection. Now, as he did so, his breath caught in his throat. The young cub he had been was gone. His mane had grown wild and long over the years and his head had become wider, his shoulders more powerful. Simba leaned down and his breath caught in his throat as he realized—he looked just like his father.

CHAPTER EIGHTEEN

"You see," Rafiki said from behind his shoulder, startling Simba. "He lives in you."

Simba didn't take his eyes off the water. While a part of him knew that it was just his own reflection, it was the closest he had come to seeing his father in a long, long time. His eyes welled and a single tear dropped into the water, disturbing the reflection.

"Simba."

Hearing his name, Simba looked up. The voice was deep, familiar. It sent a shock through him and made him shiver. As he watched, the clouds in the sky began to shift and move, coming together and transforming from shapeless white into an image of his father. Mufasa looked down on his son, his eyes wise and kind.

"Father?" Simba said in disbelief. More clouds began to race over the sky, coming together as lightning flashed and thunder rumbled. The air felt electric and smelled like rain. It was a magical feeling, one that Simba had loved when he was a cub. It meant life-giving water. It meant change and hope and transformation. And now, somehow, it meant his father.

From up in the clouds, Mufasa smiled down on his son. "Simba," he said, his voice as deep and rumbling as the thunder itself. "You must take your place in the Circle of Life."

Simba shook his head. "I can't," he said softly. Admitting the words aloud to his father was harder than it had been to admit it to Rafiki or Nala. But nothing had changed. True, his father was there with him now. But he was still dead. And Simba knew it was his fault. He couldn't disappoint his father—not again.

"You must remember who you are," Mufasa said. "The one true king."

"I'm sorry," Simba said. "I don't know how to be like you."

"As king, I was most proud of one thing," Mufasa said, his voice kind and full of nostalgia. "Having you as my son."

Mufasa's words broke Simba. A cry caught in his throat. He wanted to tell his father how desperately he had longed to hear those words. He wanted to run and jump on his back and snuggle into his mane and feel the safety and comfort he had when he was a child. He wanted so much to tell Mufasa everything and have his father forgive him and tell him it would be all right. But most of all, he wanted his father to be alive. "That was a long time ago," he finally said softly.

To his surprise, Mufasa shook his head. "No, Simba," he said. "That is forever."

The clouds began to roll faster, moving past the

moon. Mufasa's image started to move with the clouds, fading. "Please!" Simba begged, running under the moving clouds. "Don't leave me again."

"I never left you," Mufasa said. The clouds moved still farther away from the moon. The light the moon cast grew weaker, along with the vision of Mufasa. In moments, he had all but disappeared. "Remember . . . remember . . ." he said.

And then, just like that, Mufasa was gone. Simba stood under the blanket of stars—alone. Turning, he walked slowly back toward Rafiki.

"Strange weather, heh?" Rafiki said, looking up at the cloudless sky. "What did you see?"

Simba shrugged. He was flooded with too many emotions. His father had appeared to him and told him to remember who he was. The irony was he had never forgotten. He had just chosen to ignore it. Because who he had been was the reason his father was gone. What good would it do to remember? Shaking his head, he looked up at Rafiki. "Doesn't matter," he finally answered. "It's in the past."

CHAPTER EIGHTEEN

WHACK!

Simba cried out as Rafiki smacked him—hard—across the head with his wooden cane. "OW!" he cried. "What was that for?"

Rafiki shrugged. "It doesn't matter," he said. "It's in the past."

Simba scowled. He knew what Rafiki was trying to do. But it wouldn't work. "I can never be like him—" he started to say.

"And *he* could never be like you," Rafiki countered.

For a long moment, Simba just stood there, his eyes lifted to the stars. His father had told him long ago that he was never alone, that he was part of something bigger than himself. Maybe there was a reason for all this. Maybe Nala and Rafiki and his father were right. Maybe it was time to take his place in the Circle of Life. He shook his head. But how? What was he supposed to do after all this time? How could he return to a life he had run away from?

"And so, I ask again," Rafiki said, interrupting his thoughts, "who are you?"

Simba didn't have the answers—not to all of his questions. But he was done pretending he didn't know the answer to Rafiki's. Walking over, he stopped in front of the monkey. Then, lifting his head, he nodded. "I am Simba," he answered. "Son of Mufasa."

The sun was rising, a red ball illuminating the sky and torching the ground. Simba raced toward it and the clearing where he knew Nala should be. As he burst into the grassy circle, he spotted her, her back to him. Smiling, he raced over toward Nala—and then right by her.

"Sun is up!" he shouted over his shoulder. "No time to waste!"

"Wait!" Nala called after him. "Where are you going?"

Simba didn't stop as he shouted back over his shoulder. "To challenge Scar!" He hadn't realized that was what he was doing until he said the words out loud. But every moment since Nala had shown up had been leading to this inevitable point. He had to go back home. He had to try—even if he didn't succeed—to end Scar's reign.

As Nala heard his answer, her face lit up with hope. That look only encouraged him to run faster. He had already waited far too long.

As they raced away from the jungle, the green, soft ground giving way to the hard-packed, rocky dirt of the desert, Simba tried to imagine what he was going to see. When he had fled the Pride Lands years before, he had been wrapped in misery. His sadness and fear had clouded everything, and even now he barely remembered the journey. But this time, he was all too aware of the changing landscape as they came closer and closer to the Pride Lands.

Climbing over the large sand dunes, he heard thunder in the distance. The air was growing thick with an impending storm and the clouds were dark now, blocking out the sun. It gave Simba an ominous feeling, and he felt his pace slow. But looking to his side, he saw the determination on Nala's face. It spurred him on, his paws racing over the sand, up and down dunes until he saw the rise that marked the edge of the Pride Lands.

Taking a deep breath, Simba put on one last burst of speed and crested the rise. Then he stopped, looking at his home for the first time in years.

And what he saw horrified him.

Nala was right. The Pride Lands were devastated. The earth was parched, a sea of dried bones and death. Try as he might, he couldn't see a single living thing. The land he remembered as lush and full of animals was completely unrecognizable. Scar and his hyenas had ravaged it, making it a shadow of what it had once been. As Simba lifted his eyes toward Pride Rock in the distance, he swallowed heavily. Even that seemed different. Under the dark clouds that hovered in the sky, Pride Rock seemed gray, lifeless, as though its soul had left.

"I didn't want to believe you . . ." Simba said, his voice trailing off as he was overcome with emotion.

"Scar's got an army, Simba," Nala said. Her own

eyes were hard, the sight of the Pride Lands all too familiar to her.

Simba shook his head. He didn't care about an army. He couldn't get past what he saw right at that moment. "I'm sorry," he said softly. "I never imagined . . ."

Nala turned and looked at him. She nodded, her eyes tender. Then she spoke. "What are you going to do?"

It was a good question. It was the very one he had been asking himself since he'd raced away from the jungle. He hadn't known then, but now he did. He couldn't stand by and let Scar take anything else from the Pride Lands. Rafiki had asked him who he was. Well, he was Mufasa's son. And Mufasa would never just walk away from this. Taking a deep breath, he looked out over the plain. "Everything the light touches is my kingdom," he said. "If I don't fight for it, who will?"

"I will," Nala replied.

Simba looked over at her and smiled. But then his smile faded. "It's going to be dangerous," he warned.

Nala laughed. "Danger?" she said, a twinkle in her eye. "Ha! I laugh in the face of danger! Ha! Ha! Ha!"

Hearing the words he had spoken years ago when he was so young was just what Simba needed. In that moment, the tension broke and the two friends began to laugh. It didn't matter that there was a twinge of hysteria and fear to the laughter; it soothed both their souls. For the first time since they had been reunited, Simba felt like he and Nala were back to where they should be. A team. Best friends who would have each other's backs no matter what. Protect each other through thick and—

Suddenly, a strange sound broke the moment.

Turning, Simba and Nala watched as a shape appeared on the horizon. Simba squinted, trying to make out exactly what it was. An animal of sorts? It was round—ish. And tall—ish. But also sort of squarish. And it seemed to have three—or maybe four?—heads. Just then, the shape burst out of the shadows, and Simba let out a cry of recognition.

It wasn't one animal . . . it was four! Pumbaa was

running toward them as fast as his warthog legs could carry him. Riding atop his head was Timon, his arm raised high. And on Pumbaa's back sat the bush baby and the elephant shrew. Behind them came the honey badger.

"What are you guys doing here?" Simba said when they stopped, breathless, in front of him.

"Dying would be my first guess," the honey badger answered.

"I don't recommend riding on the back of a wart-hog," piped up the bush baby, his wide eyes even wider than usual and his big ears flipping back and forth frantically. He crinkled his nose. "I've been holding my breath since the gorge."

Simba bit back a laugh as Pumbaa shot the bush baby a look. He was so glad to see his friends, but he still didn't understand what they were doing there. Why would they risk running toward a place they didn't know to help fight an enemy they had never seen? When Simba pressed them for an answer, Timon and Pumbaa—well, mostly Pumbaa—pointed out that they were friends. And friends stuck together. End of story.

"We are at your service, my liege!" Pumbaa said, bowing.

Timon, who had been oddly quiet, pushed past Simba and Nala and looked over the ridge toward the plains below. He raised an eyebrow. "So," he said, "*this* is the place you're fighting for?"

"Yes, Timon," Simba said. "This is my home." Saying the word aloud made everything seem more real. A renewed sense of urgency filled him and he began to pace, eager to get going.

But Timon was on a roll. "Talk about your fixer-upper! I like what you've done with it—a bit heavy on the carcass."

Ignoring his friend, Pumbaa pushed forward. "Simba, we're with you to the end," he said solemnly. "Just tell us what to do."

Simba stopped pacing. Looking at his friends, he smiled. Scar might have an army, but he had these guys. And when it came to a fight, he wouldn't want to have anyone else behind him. Turning, he gazed out at the dark clouds and the devastated Pride Rock. It was time to put an end to Scar's rule.

CHAPTER NINETEEN

Simba was beginning to think he might have bitten off more than he could chew.

Together, he and the others had made it safely across the plains without being spotted. Simba had been anxious that the hyenas would smell his scent, but he must have been lucky. He and his friends were able to get all the way to the bottom of Pride Rock without a single encounter with one of the slobbery, smelly creatures.

But then their luck ran out.

Ducking behind a large rock, Simba, Nala, and the others paused to take stock of the situation. Slowly, Simba lifted his head and peered over the edge of the rock. He groaned and lowered back down. Two large hyenas were guarding the entrance to Pride Rock. And while most of the hyenas Simba had dealt with had dull eyes to match their dim brains and dingy bodies, these two hyenas looked bigger and tougher than the rest.

"We're dead," the bush baby said when Simba gave his report.

"Looking back, I wasted so much time on grooming," the elephant shrew added, his long nose twitching nervously.

Shoving the others aside, Timon leaned in close to Simba. "What's your plan for getting past the slobbering guards?" he asked, getting to the point.

Simba's eyes narrowed. He peeked back over the rock once more. Then he sat back and looked around at his friends. His gaze landed on Pumbaa. The warthog was busily rubbing at an itch on his round, meaty hindquarters. Simba smiled. It seemed he did, in fact, have a plan. "Live bait," he said.

Following his gaze, the others looked at Pumbaa. Oblivious, Pumbaa looked up from his itching. "Great idea!" he said genuinely. "Those guys would never resist fresh meat! Now all we have to do is find something plump and juicy!" He paused, looking thoughtful. "Maybe a gnu?"

Simba shook his head.

"No gnu?" Pumbaa said, suddenly looking a bit nervous as he realized everyone was staring at him a little too intensely.

"It's you," Timon said.

Pumbaa gulped. Simba tried to smile reassuringly, but he knew that Pumbaa had just been nominated for a job he didn't want. Still, it was their only hope of getting past the hyenas. Quickly, they came up with a plan. It was simple: Timon and Pumbaa would distract the hyenas by walking in front of them. And with the guards preoccupied with the warthog and the meerkat, Simba and Nala would run as fast as they could through the entrance and up to Pride Rock.

Simple.

In theory.

But none of them could have taken into account just how hungry—and surprisingly fast—the hyenas would be. Or how dramatic Timon could be. Jumping out from behind the rock, Timon stood up like an auctioneer and began his sale. "Are you achin' for some bacon?" he called out. Immediately, the two hyenas turned and looked over to where a very nervous Pumbaa stood. "Want to dine on some tasty swine? Step right up and get in line! Who's hungry?" Timon had barely finished before the hyenas began drooling. And then—they came barreling toward them.

"RUN!" Timon shouted.

Pumbaa didn't need to be told twice. He took off and sprinted away, screaming, the hyenas close behind.

Simba and Nala waited until the hyenas had passed them and then quickly made their way over to the entrance to Pride Rock. Taking a deep breath, Simba looked over at Nala. She nodded.

It was time to save the Pride Lands.

Scar looked out at the approaching storm. Lifting his head, he breathed in deeply. He had always liked a good storm. The electricity. The danger. The darkness. He knew storms put the lionesses on edge and had heard Sarabi's endless warnings that the next storm could set the dry and dead plains ablaze. But he ignored those warnings, the same way he ignored all the lionesses' complaints.

Turning his attention from the impending storm, he looked over to where Sarabi lay on the hard stone of Pride Rock. Her body was weak, her head heavy and her breathing labored. The days since Nala had left had been hard on her and the others. Scar had punished them all for Nala's betrayal, feeding them only scraps—if the hyenas left any.

"Sarabi," he said, walking over. "Seeing you hungry breaks my heart. You can't live off scraps for much longer." While his words were caring, his tone was not. It was cold, just like his eyes. As he came closer, Sarabi struggled to her feet, the effort exhausting her. She swayed for a moment, trying to get her balance. "All you have to do is be my queen," he said.

The lioness shook her head. "It's over, Scar," she said weakly. "Don't you see that?"

Scar's eyes narrowed. He was growing tired of this conversation and Sarabi's stubborn answers. "You're suffering for what?" he snarled. "The memory of a life you once knew. A king you once loved."

"Still love," Sarabi answered.

"I tried to make you understand what a true king can be!" Scar said, growing angrier by the minute.

But Sarabi didn't seem to care. Lifting her head and looking him right in the eye, she spoke softly and with conviction. "A true king's power is his compassion."

Scar let out an angry roar. He had had enough. For years he had watched Sarabi belittle him, undermining his authority and denying his advances. He had watched her pine for Mufasa like a lovesick cub and seen the power of that love keep her going when others wanted to run. While he would never admit it out loud, she was a queen, through and through. And stronger than he had ever imagined. But he was not going to stand it any longer. She was too much of a liability. She would bow to him—or die. His body vibrating with rage, he stalked closer. "I am TEN times the king Mufasa was!" he screamed. "And I will prove it with my own claws!"

Lightning flashed in the air as he lifted one of his paws. Thunder boomed and Pride Rock trembled. But as the thunder faded, it turned into a roar. Looking up, Scar widened his eyes in fear.

Standing on a rock above them, illuminated by the flashes of lightning, was the shadowy figure of a lion.

"Move away from her, Scar," the lion said.

"Mufasa," Scar whispered. "It can't be . . ."

Behind him, he heard Sarabi's sharp intake of breath. "Simba . . ."

Looking up once more, Scar narrowed his eyes as

the lion jumped down in front of them. He shook his head, trying to make sense of it all. Sarabi was right. It was Simba. Fully grown and the spitting image of his father, with the brawn and ferocity to match.

Slowly, Scar began to back away.

"You're alive? How can that be?"

At the sound of his mother's smooth voice, Simba nearly cried. He had never thought he would see her again. Yet here they both were. Walking over, he nuzzled his head against hers. It felt familiar and strange at the same time. When he had left, his head had barely reached her knee; now he had to bend to meet her.

"It doesn't matter," Simba said, finally pulling himself away. "I'm home."

"Simba," Scar said, his voice breaking the moment. "I'm so happy to see you. *Alive.*"

Turning, Simba looked over at his uncle. While his mother looked thin and weak, Scar looked well-fed and rested. Simba narrowed his eyes. "Give me one good reason why I shouldn't rip you apart!"

"I can give you more than one," Scar said. He nodded over his shoulder. While Simba and his mother had been reuniting, the hyenas had gathered. Now they came from every corner of Pride Rock, their lips pulled back in snarls, their hackles raised. "You see, they think *I'm* king," he said with a shrug.

Simba looked at the growing number of hyenas. He shifted nervously on his feet. Nala had told him to be prepared for the hyenas, and he had seen them in number back in the Elephant Graveyard all those years ago. But now, face to face with them, Simba grew worried.

"Simba is the rightful king!"

At the sound of Nala's voice, Simba turned. She had gone and gathered the other lionesses while he was with his mother. They now stood behind her, their strength renewed as they saw Simba for the first time.

Emboldened once more, Simba turned back to Scar. "The choice is yours, Scar," he said. "Step down or fight."

"Must this all end in violence?" Scar said, always the politician. "I'd hate to be responsible for the death of a family member. To feel the shame of knowing I took the life of someone I loved." He stopped, raising an eyebrow at Simba as if daring him to argue.

Simba shook his head. He wasn't going to let Scar talk his way out of this. "I've put all that behind me—" he started to say.

"But have they put it behind them?" Scar interrupted. He gestured to the gathered lionesses. "Do your faithful subjects know what you've done?"

"What is he talking about?" Nala said, looking back and forth between Simba and Scar.

Simba looked over at Nala. She stared back, a look of doubt creeping into her eyes. He bit back a groan. He should have told her the truth back in the jungle. He should have known that Scar would use his past against him. But he had been scared, and he hadn't wanted to see the uncertainty in her eyes—the same uncertainty he saw now. He opened his mouth, wishing for the words to come, but they didn't.

Instead, Scar went on. “Well, Simba,” he said, clearly enjoying the moment. “Now’s your chance to confess. Tell them who’s responsible for Mufasa’s death.”

All eyes turned to Simba. He felt each one like a lead weight on his back. He sighed. There was no use pretending anymore. Scar was right. If Simba wanted to be king, the lionesses needed to know the truth. “It was me,” he said.

“No,” Sarabi said, shaking her head. “You were a cub! This can’t be true.”

Meeting her eyes, Simba nodded. “It’s true,” he said, his heart breaking as he watched his mother’s face crumple. “I’m so sorry.”

“He admits it!” Scar shouted, unconcerned with the moment unfolding between mother and son. “Murderer!”

Out over the Pride Lands, the storm grew fiercer. Lightning flashed, and thunder boomed. As Simba hung his head in shame, the lightning came faster and faster, approaching Pride Rock as though laying judgment on him. Suddenly, one of the flashes struck the ground at the bottom of the rock. In an instant, the dry, dead grass burst into flame.

Unaware of the growing fire below, Simba looked up. His head swung between his mother and Nala and the other lionesses. "It was an accident," he said, his voice sounding small. *I didn't mean to hurt him.* An image of his father falling flashed in front of his eyes.

Scar sneered. "If it weren't for you, the king would be alive," he said, each word landing like a blow to Simba's heart. "It's your fault he is dead! Do you deny it?"

"No."

The single word reverberated over Pride Rock, louder than the thunder above.

CHAPTER TWENTY

The air crackled with tension as the lionesses and hyenas watched uncle and nephew. On the ground below, the fire grew bigger, the flames rising up and tickling the top of Pride Rock. But Simba was oblivious to the heat and the danger. All he could hear was his own pounding heart, and all he could feel was the horrified looks of the lionesses.

"You're guilty!" Scar screamed at him.

Simba shook his head. "I'm not a murderer!"

he cried. *I'm not!* he added silently. *I didn't mean for any of it to happen. It was an accident. A terrible, terrible accident.* But the words stayed locked inside him, unable to escape. He bowed his head and lowered his shoulders, as if trying to hide inside himself.

"We should believe a son who takes the life of a king?" Scar said. He turned and looked at Sarabi. "A son who abandons his own mother!" Stalking forward, Scar reached out a paw and swiped it across Simba's face.

"No! I'm—I'm—" Simba struggled to explain.

"You're what?" Scar sneered. "Say it! Are you the king? ARE YOU THE KING?" Once again, he reached out and hit Simba.

As he felt Scar's paw across his face, pushing him back toward the edge of the rock, Simba cowered. Over and over again, Scar swiped at him, and each time, a flash of that horrible day overcame him, making Simba grow weaker. It was as though he were a small cub again, unable to do anything to stop the horror happening in front of him. He saw Mufasa clinging to the rocks, trying to live. His powerful muscles rippling as he struggled and then the horrible moment when he disappeared into the stampede.

"You're what?" Scar pushed. "Say it!"

Another image of his father flashed in his mind. Mufasa, looking out over his kingdom, the sun on his mane and his eyes wide—every inch the king Simba could never be. "I'm—I'm—nothing," Simba said.

Letting out a roar of triumph, Scar hit him one last time, the motion sending Simba flying off the rock. As he fell back toward the fire, he heard Nala scream his name. Instinctively, he reached out and grabbed at the rocky side. He could hear the crackle of the approaching fire below. Desperately, he clung to the edge.

Above him, Scar's face appeared. In the light from the fire, his scar was even more pronounced. He looked down at Simba—and then he smiled. "Now, this looks familiar," he said. "Where have I seen this before? Oh, yes, I remember. This is the way Mufasa looked before he died. I looked down—saw the fear in his eyes . . ." He paused, leaning over so only Simba could hear his next words. "And here's *my* little secret: I killed Mufasa."

Simba's head snapped back. His eyes met Scar's and, in that instant, he knew what had happened. Simba hadn't killed his father. Scar had. Scar had had the chance to save his brother, and instead, he had let him fall. Just like he was going to let Simba fall now.

Rage flooded through Simba, and before he could even think about what he was doing, he let out a roar. With all his remaining strength, he lunged forward, biting into Scar's mane.

Shocked, Scar pulled back, taking Simba with him. As they tumbled back onto Pride Rock, Simba got to his feet and charged, hitting Scar head-on, his momentum fueled by adrenaline and the life he had missed out on because of Scar's betrayal. "My father!" he shouted. "Your own brother! How could you?"

Scar backed up. Looking at the lionesses, he tried to keep the charade going. "First he kills Mufasa, and now he wants to kill me!"

"YOU KILLED HIM!" Simba screamed. "TELL THEM THE TRUTH!"

Scar shook his head. "Don't believe his lies."

"Scar." Sarabi's voice was loud, even over the thunder and the encroaching flames. She stepped forward so she was close to Simba. Looking at his mother, Simba saw that the disappointment was gone from her eyes. Her eyes looked clear—and angry. "You told us you didn't get to the gorge in time," she said, each word measured.

"Yes," Scar said. "That's true!"

Sarabi's eyes narrowed. "Then how did you see the look in Mufasa's eyes?" she asked.

Simba began to smile as Scar's face fell. He was caught. Sarabi was right. There was no way he could have seen Mufasa's eyes if he hadn't been there when the king died. Everything Scar had told them was a lie. Everything he had told Simba was a lie. He had been the reason Simba ran away, the reason the Pride Lands were destroyed. He was the reason Mufasa was dead.

"MURDERER!" Simba said, echoing Scar's own words back at him.

For one long moment, Scar stood rooted to the spot. Simba stared at him, his body pulsing with triumph and rage. But then a smile spread over Scar's face. Looking behind him, he gestured to the hyenas. "Kill them all!"

In an instant, Pride Rock was full of the sounds of snarling and snapping as lions and hyenas faced off. With a roar, Simba dove into the fray, tossing hyenas aside one by one as they came after him. Beside him, Nala and Sarabi fought, eagerly tearing into the creatures that had made their lives miserable for so long.

Smoke filled the air as the fire below grew closer, casting hyenas into shadow as they charged and were flung head over tail back toward the rocks and the ground below. Through it all, Simba kept his eyes locked on Scar. His uncle was backing away, trying to escape. Pushing through a group of hyenas, Simba paused as he caught sight of his mother. Shenzi and her pack were moving in on the queen, their jaws snapping.

Simba hesitated, not sure what to do. He didn't want to leave his mother, but Scar was inching farther and farther away. Just then, he heard a familiar sound. A moment later, Pumbaa charged headfirst into the hyenas surrounding Sarabi, bowling them over the way he did with vultures. On Pumbaa's back, Timon let out a triumphant cry. "That never gets old!" the meerkat shouted.

As Timon and Pumbaa continued to take down hyenas, Simba turned to go after Scar. He ducked and weaved as he went, just missing the slashing claws and snapping jaws of the hyenas. With every move, he looked more and more like Mufasa. The transformation was enough to send some hyenas yipping away at the mere sight of him. But Simba was only after Scar. The older lion kept moving, trying to escape.

Behind him, Simba heard the other animals from the jungle join in the fight. He heard yelps as his friends used their tusks, teeth, and speed, joining the lionesses to push the hyenas back until soon they were all running for their lives. He could hear triumphant shouts from the lionesses as the hyenas fled.

But Simba didn't have time to revel in the reclamation of Pride Rock. He needed to get to Scar. He wasn't going to let the lion get away. But the air had grown black with smoke, making it nearly impossible to see. Blindly, Simba pushed his way through the curtain of ash. Just then, a flash of lightning illuminated the spot right in front of Simba. In that moment, he saw Scar. The older lion was hunched over, creeping his way closer to the steep incline that would lead him to the top of Pride Rock.

Letting out a roar of rage, Simba pounced, landing mere inches from his uncle. "It's over, Scar," he said, his voice deep.

Slowly, Scar turned to face Simba. Holding up his paws, he tried to look innocent. "Simba, have mercy. I beg you."

Simba raised an eyebrow. "Mercy?" he repeated. "After what you did?"

"It was the hyenas!" Scar said desperately. "Those revolting scavengers made me do it! I was planning on killing them all—"

Behind him, Simba heard the remaining hyenas let out angry snarls. For once, the sound didn't anger him or bother him. In fact, he felt a sudden kinship with the creatures. "You fooled the hyenas," he said. "Just like you fooled me." As he spoke, he moved forward, forcing Scar to back up the steep path. The older lion's feet scrambled on the hard stone, but Simba kept stalking forward until they reached the very top of Pride Rock.

Scar cowered at the edge of the rock and looked over at Simba, his eyes filled with genuine fear. "Simba, you wouldn't kill your only uncle . . ." he said hopefully.

Simba didn't hesitate. Moving quickly, he went to strike Scar. He never wanted to see the lion's face again. But just before he hit him, Simba stopped. If he were to push Scar over the edge, how would he be any better than his uncle? His father had taught him to be a strong, wise king. Killing Scar wouldn't be an act of strength, it would be an act of revenge. He shook his head. "No, Scar," he finally said. "I'm not like you."

A smile came over Scar's face. "Oh, Simba," Scar said, groveling now that his death wasn't imminent. "You are truly noble! And I will make it up to you—just tell me how I can prove myself! Tell me what you want me to do!"

Simba paused. Then, slowly, he leaned in. "Run," he said, repeating the words Scar had said to him all those years ago. "Run away and never return."

For a long moment, Scar just looked at Simba, as if seeing the ghost of his brother. Finally, he nodded. "Yes, of course," Scar said, bowing his head. "As you wish . . . Your Majesty." But no sooner had the words left his mouth than he reached down and scooped up a pile of hot embers. With a snarl, he threw them at Simba, momentarily blinding him.

As Simba swiped at his burning eyes, Scar jumped at him, knocking him back to the ground. Simba felt the air rush from his lungs as his uncle tried to pin him to the rock. Simba roared loudly, pushing back.

He had offered Scar a chance and his uncle had literally thrown it away. Anger fueled him as he fought back, blindly swinging at his uncle.

Thunder continued to roll as the two wrestled and tumbled across the rock, fighting fiercely. Below them, the remaining hyenas and the pride of lionesses watched anxiously. Unaware of the audience or anything but his traitorous uncle, Simba fought with all he had. He fought for the years and hopes he had lost. He fought for the moments he would never get back—with his mother, with Nala, with his father. But most importantly, he fought with the heart of a king. With one final roar, he pushed Scar back and shot to his feet.

"You can't win, Scar," Simba said, his chest heaving.

"This is *my* kingdom," Scar said, his own breath heavy. "*My* destiny!" Letting out a roar of his own, he charged one more time.

But unlike before, this time Simba was prepared. Quickly, he stepped to the side, avoiding the charging lion. Scar rushed past him and right over the edge of the rock. He fell through the air, landing with a thud on the ground far below.

Simba raced to the edge and peered over the side of the cliff. Below, he could see his uncle slowly and painfully getting to his feet. A group of hyenas, led by Shenzi, slowly encircled him. Even from his vantage point high up on the top of Pride Rock, Simba could see that the hyenas had had enough of their "leader." They had heard him call them scavengers. They had heard his plan to be done with them. Hyenas weren't the brightest animals, but Simba knew they weren't forgiving, either. As he turned to walk back down to the lionesses, Simba heard Scar's frightened shouts and the snarls of the hyenas. They would teach Scar a lesson—one he would certainly never forget.

Simba walked slowly, his body aching. In the sky above, the clouds opened and rain began to fall, drenching his coat and dousing the raging fires that had been engulfing Pride Rock. Emerging at the bottom of the path, Simba walked out onto the flat rock he could once again call home.

A smile spread across his face as he looked around. Sarabi and Nala stood waiting for him, surrounded by the other lionesses. And off to one side, happy but still slightly nervous to be around so many carnivores, Timon, Pumbaa, and the others stood smiling, too. Simba walked over to Sarabi and nuzzled her. Then he turned and gave a nod of thanks to his friends. Timon waved happily and did a little dance while Pumbaa did what he did best: he passed gas. Laughing, Simba finally turned to Nala. There was so much he wanted to say to her. So many things he *should* have said. He wanted to thank her—for saving him. But as he looked into her eyes, the words got lodged in his throat. Instead, ever so gently, he stretched out his neck until their noses just barely touched. It wasn't everything, but it was a start to something so much more.

Unable to stop smiling, he turned at the sound of flapping wings. Looking up, he saw Zazu. The hornbill landed in front of him and bowed. "Your Majesty," he said.

Simba inclined his head. But before he could greet his old friend, he saw Rafiki standing near the promontory of Pride Rock. The mandrill gestured at Simba with his wooden staff. With another nod at his friends—old and new—Simba slowly walked over to Rafiki. Pointing his cane toward the end of the promontory, the old monkey said nothing. But he didn't need to. Simba knew what to do. It was in his blood.

Lifting his head, he walked to the very edge of Pride Rock. He stopped and gazed up at the sky. The storm had gone, taking the rain, dark clouds, and thunder with it. In its place, a field of stars had emerged, their twinkling lights illuminating the night. As he stared up at the familiar sky, Simba heard his father's voice on the wind. "Remember . . ." Mufasa said.

I'll never forget, Simba vowed silently. He was king now and forever. And he would spend his life making sure he lived up to his father's wishes. He would be the mightiest king he could be. And he would remember—everything and everyone who had gotten him to this place.

Tilting back his head, Simba let out a roar.

On the rock behind him, Nala, Sarabi, and the other lionesses let out resounding roars. The sound echoed out from Pride Rock and over the lands beyond. Simba smiled as he looked out over his kingdom. The past was in the past. Timon and Pumbaa were right about that. Now it was time to look toward the future.

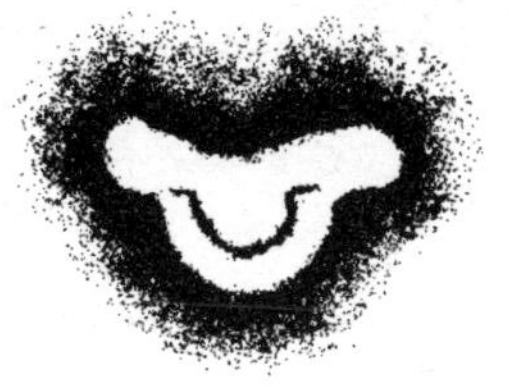

EPILOGUE

Simba stared out at the plains in front of him. Herds of elephants moved across the savannah, babies hanging on to their mothers' tails. Topis and gazelles jumped through the lush, thick grass, their horns glistening in the sun. Simba could hear the loud calls of the hippos from the watering hole as they emerged from under the water and sprayed unsuspecting drinkers. In the trees, mandrills chittered and called to each other, swinging from branch to branch to greet friends and family. The long-necked giraffes ambled along slowly, stopping to graze on branches loaded with vibrant, life-giving leaves. The air was sweet with the scent of life, the plains no longer the ravished wasteland they had been under Scar's rule.

Life had returned to the Pride Lands.

Turning, Simba walked back toward his den. A smile broke over his face as he saw his young son playing with Timon and Pumbaa. Nala looked on, her eyes full of love and wonder as she gazed at the cub. Sensing Simba's eyes on her, she looked up and smiled proudly.

Hearing the unmistakable sound of Rafiki's staff hitting the hard rock, Simba gestured for Nala to join him. Picking up their cub, she walked over to him, and together, they followed Rafiki up to the promontory. Below, the animals had gathered to once again honor their future king.

As Rafiki held up the cub, Simba turned to look at Nala and smiled. Years before, he had run away and thought he could never return. But his father had been right. Life was a circle. And he had always been a part of it. He had just needed a little nudge to remember.

Below, the animals let out cries of joy as they welcomed the new cub. Simba slowly backed up. He had time yet, but someday, this kingdom would be his child's. Until then, he would do his best to honor his promise to Mufasa. Simba would always remember who he was, and who Mufasa had been. And no matter what path his child found, he would be there. And he would also be there for Nala, for his friends, and for his kingdom. That was Simba's path.